EX LIB

VINTAGE **CLASSICS**

VITA SACKVILLE-WEST

Victoria Mary Sackville-West, known as Vita, was born in 1892 at Knole in Kent, the only child of aristocratic parents. In 1913 she married diplomat Harold Nicolson, with whom she had two sons and travelled extensively before settling at Sissinghurst Castle in 1930, where she devoted much of her time to creating its now world-famous garden. Throughout her life Sackville-West had a number of other relationships with both men and women, and her unconventional marriage would later become the subject of a biography written by her son Nigel Nicolson. Though she produced a substantial body of work, amongst which are writings on travel and gardening, Sackville-West is best known for her novels *The Edwardians* (1930) and *All Passion Spent* (1931), and for the pastoral poem *The Land* (1926) which was awarded the prestigious Hawthornden Prize. She died in 1962 at Sissinghurst.

ALSO BY VITA SACKVILLE-WEST

Novels

Family History
Heritage
The Dragon in Shallow Waters
The Heir
Challenge
Seducers in Ecuador
The Edwardians
All Passion Spent

Non-Fiction

Passenger to Teheran
Saint Joan of Arc
English Country Houses
Pepita
The Eagle and The Dove
Sissinghurst: The Creation of a Garden

VITA SACKVILLE-WEST

Grand Canyon

VINTAGE

2 4 6 8 10 9 7 5 3 1

Vintage
20 Vauxhall Bridge Road,
London SW1V 2SA

Vintage Classics is part of the Penguin Random House
group of companies whose addresses can be found at
global.penguinrandomhouse.com.

Penguin
Random House
UK

First published in Great Britain by Michael Joseph Ltd in 1942
This edition reissued by Vintage in 2018

penguin.co.uk/vintage

A CIP catalogue record for this book is available from the British Library

ISBN 9781784873493

Printed and bound by Clays Ltd, St Ives plc

Penguin Random House is committed to a sustainable future for
our business, our readers and our planet. This book is made
from Forest Stewardship Council® certified paper.

CONTENTS

★

AUTHOR'S NOTE

IN Grand Canyon *I have intended a caution-
ary tale. In it I have contemplated the dangers of a world in which Germany, by the use
of an unspecified method of attack, is assumed
to have defeated Great Britain in the present
war. Peace terms have been offered on the basis
of the status quo of 1939 and the Germans
have made a plausible appeal to the United States
Government (who have meanwhile satisfactorily
concluded their own war with Japan) to mediate
in the name of humanity to prevent a prolongation
of human suffering. For the purposes of my story
I have allowed the United States Government to
fall into the Nazi trap and to be deluded into
making this intervention as "the nation which,
in its hour of victory, brought peace to the world."
The terrible consequences of an incomplete conclusion or indeed of any peace signed by the Allies
with an undefeated Germany are shown.*

*Such a supposition is by no means intended as a
prophecy and indeed bears no relation at all to
my own views as to the outcome of the present war.*

V. S.-W.

Part One

★

THE HOTEL

MR. DALE had seen Mrs. Temple daily, including her among the other hotel guests. There were as usual a number of people staying in the hotel on the edge of the canyon, even more than usual this year, owing to the manœuvres. This time he really saw her for the first time, talking to an Indian boy with a pony, out in the desert. She talked earnestly and quickly, having orders to give and he orders to fulfil, and both of them some consultation to take with one another. The boy standing beside his pony nodded rapidly, ready to be off. They made a contrast with one another under the strong sunlight of the desert, she the European, he the Indian, she light, he dark, she in her flowery muslin, he in his red shirt and fringed trousers of tanned hide, she with a sunshade like a bubble above her head, he with his black hair bound by a scarlet band.

Then he was gone, in the instant he bestrode his pony. He became part of the desert, a Centaur speck of boy and horse, he crouching low over the mane, native, going off on the unknown mission given to him by the European woman.

So she has a life of her own? She talks with Indian boys and gives them their instructions. She is not just a hotel guest among other hotel guests? What then is she? Who is Sylvia, what is she?

> "Fairer than Isaac's lover at the well,
> She that in chains of pearl and unicorn
> Leads at her train the ancient golden world." . . .

The climate of his mind was composed of such small scraps of beauty, though he carefully concealed the fact from everyone and even instantly corrected the weakness in his private heart. Thus, although this sudden vision of Mrs. Temple had given him so intense a pleasure that it had caused him to whisper the lines to himself, a trick he had acquired during many years spent in solitude with no one else to speak to, he immediately came back to realism with the reflection that she was not especially fair, nor even especially young. She is a woman in her middle years, staying as inexplicably as any other person in an hotel; a woman who, perhaps, has no fixed home. Every evening she dines alone at a little table, reading a book propped open by a fork. There is nothing to mark her out as different from any other tourist. Why then does she come out into the desert with her sunshade and speak so urgently to an Indian boy? She has a private existence which has no connexion with the hotel. Her name, as may be discovered from the visitors' book, is Mrs. Temple, first name, Helen. Her address is given as London. London was large once, and vague as an address. Her occupation she has left blank. She has no occupation. There is nothing more to be learnt about her.

There she goes, returning towards the hotel. She returns at a leisurely pace—and, indeed, the sun is hot and the day made for leisure; she returns, having disposed of her business with the Indian boy and despatched him off on his mission into the Painted Desert. She returns towards the hotel, following the winding path which will lead her under the pine-trees along the edge of the canyon. It is a fantastic place to watch any woman, to eavesdrop on any woman unaware that she is under observation. The human figure is dwarfed here by the extravagance of nature. It is easy to observe a woman gleaning in a cornfield, throwing out her rake and drawing it back in a gesture older than the Bible; but what is one to make of a woman wandering between the desert and the canyon? She seems to have come out of nothing and to belong to nothing.

The boy was gone; Mrs. Temple alone returned, tranquil, having given her orders. She returned, to resume her life as an hotel-guest. Lester Dale watched her go. He was not particularly interested in Mrs. Temple, not more interested in her, except for the moment, than in anyone else, for he was not particularly interested in anyone, man or woman; not even in himself. A vague speculation was the most that ever tickled his fancy. Indifference ruled his life. Places interested him more than people; but when he met with the combination of place and person, as he did now watching Mrs. Temple strolling along the edge of the canyon, his amusement was aroused. He liked to spin a tale, however little it might approach the truth. And any number of tales could be spun with the canyon as their background; the Indians themselves had turned it into the abode of legend: the spirits of the living came from it, they said, and the spirits of the dead descended into it as the entrance to the underworld, not to mention the race of little horses which were said to live at the bottom.

But Mrs. Temple—what was *she* doing there? She was a woman of culture and sophistication; an elegant woman. Not fashionable; nothing so shallow; but truly elegant of mind as of body. All her movements showed that, as well as her smile. Moreover, she was alone. No husband or lover kept her company. She was more than alone, she was extremely detached, as isolated as a figure living within a globe of glass. He had an idea that no real sound ever reached her from outside. She smiled, she laid aside her book to talk to the college girls who pestered her with adoration, she was charming, amiable, she had a friendly word always for the little waitress who had come here to Arizona because she was consumptive and loved the flowers of the desert; she could be civil even to the smart manager and his acolyte the urbane reception-clerk who inspired Lester Dale with nothing but a mild desire to push them both over the edge of the canyon. Yes, Mrs. Temple could be amiable, friendly, civil to all without ever impairing her real detachment, without ever making herself cheap and easy in the usual manner of most amiable, friendly, and civil people. That, in his eyes, was an achievement.

He had been leaning with his back against a pine-tree; now, having lost Mrs. Temple from sight, he shoved himself away from the trunk and idly followed her along the path soft with pine-needles. He could see her sunshade swelling on that narrow path above the edge of the canyon. A false step, and she would go over. Her elegance was poised precariously between the path laid by a considerate civilization and the chasm cut by inconsiderate nature.

He preferred the chasm to the path. He had seen many strange places on earth, but none so strange as this. Every year, in the course of a desultory life, he came back to it, knowing it in all seasons and by all lights. Like the Indians, he could believe that the canyon held the secrets of life and death.

It amused him to observe the various people who strayed to its rim in order to gape and wonder and exclaim. The spectacle of human vulgarity, confronted with that majesty, provoked him to a grim entertainment. Unlike Mrs. Temple, so friendly with the college girls, so benevolent towards the young lovers, he could establish no contact with them, nor was he aware of any desire to do so; and that, possibly, provided part of the pleasure he had in watching Mrs. Temple at her game of skilful management between personal immunity and human friendliness, for, like many another, he appreciated to the point of over-estimation the gifts he did not himself possess. This inability to establish ordinary contact, however, this lack of desire to do so, could not rob him of his pleasure in the spectacle of his fellow-beings at their antics. Their antics appeared especially diverting on the rim of a chasm ten miles wide and one mile deep.

He could always count on finding a parade worthy to divert him. The characters might vary in detail, but in essence they were always very much the same: muddled, inconsequent, and incomplete. Lester Dale liked his specimens to be muddled, inconsequent, and incomplete. He had persuaded himself that he successfully avoided being any of those things.

They always performed their antics very comprehensively at the hotel. This time there were the young lovers, anonymous, free French, who might as well have been at the North Pole for all they noticed of the world outside themselves. There was the baby stumbling out for a walk every morning along that precarious path. There was the blind man who had to be led. There was the deaf man whose world of silence was impenetrable. There was the consumptive waitress whose hours of freedom were few. There was the young poet whose appreciation of the external world was manifestly nil—why then had he come here to the canyon, where the external world was more overwhelming than anywhere else?—but whose preoccupation with the sufferings of his fellow-men caused him an intense, a continuous pain. There was the Polish woman. Mr. Dale disliked and mistrusted the Polish woman. There was the rabble of travellers arriving every morning and departing every night. A mixed bag. There were the college girls, going out daily with knapsacks as though they carried all the promises of life parcelled upon their backs. And there was Mrs. Temple, who belonged nowhere, yet who could send an Indian boy at full gallop out into the Painted Desert.

She worried Lester Dale. Without knowing her at all

or anything about her beyond her name, she had managed to make him feel that she understood life better than he did, and in quite as detached a way.

Having nothing better to do, he followed her at a distance. She walked slowly, in fact she strolled, as though the urgency of the message she had despatched into the desert were now a thing of the past, completed and dismissed from her mind. He admired her power of dismissal, a masculine trait estimable in so feminine a woman. She knew better than to fidget; most women were born fidgeters, one reason why he found them beyond his short patience. She strolled as though she were now given up entirely to quiet enjoyment and contemplation. He had no scruples in thus observing a woman unaware that she was under observation. It never occurred to him that some people might call him indiscreet and inquisitive. On the contrary (he would have explained), my interest is shot with admiration. He remembered a legend of the Empress Eugénie walking across the Piazzetta at Venice; how nothing could be seen of her person because of the crowds surrounding her; nothing could be seen but the bubble of her sunshade preserving its steady unvarying level above the dipping bobbing bubbles of other women's less Imperial gait. Helen Temple walks like that. Here on the rim of the canyon she walks alone, but in a crowd she would walk with the same serenity. In any circumstance of pomp or danger she would still walk with the same serenity.

How do I know these things about her? I know them, now that I have perceived her for the first time. I am watching her now and I suddenly know more about her than if she had been my wife, my sister or my mistress for twenty years.

He continued to follow her. She wandered on, leaving the pine-trees behind her and the soft path of pine-needles, passing the hotel and wandering on towards the stark splendour of the canyon. She paused there for a lonely moment, but then the college boys and girls appeared riding up on a string of mules. Lester Dale watched them meeting Mrs. Temple at the head of Bright Angel Trail. He and Mrs. Temple were both English. It amused him to watch his compatriot meeting American youth at the head of the trail.

He wondered what had happened to all of them down there. It must be a strange experience to go a mile down into the earth. What had they learnt there, all those youths and girls? Adolescent youth. Had they learnt something about life and possibly sex down there? Bright Angel Trail—splendid words. The trail of the bright deceptive angel. Had they learnt something unforgettable down there, something important yet unimportant, the expense of spirit in a waste of shame? Lester Dale had a realistic mind. Sex had never bothered him much; but that lucky escape did not prevent him from speculating on the sex life of other people. Those adolescents. Co-ed. Fraternity; sorority. Phi-Kappa-delta. Boys and girls. Animal nature, human nature. What use had they made of it at the bottom of the canyon, that dangerous place? Adonis' gardens, that one day bloomed and fruitful were the next. What was Mrs. Temple saying to the college boys and girls now that she had met them at the head of Bright Angel Trail?

He stopped behind a pine-tree to watch her intercepted by the gay train of boys and girls.

The boys came up out of the canyon and rode away at once, to get away alone by themselves from women. They had got themselves up in cowboy dress, open shirt necks, big hats and fringed chaps, because it was the romantic thing to do. The touch of the dude ranch had laid itself on their shoulders. But they had had enough of romance and women for the day and were relieved to leave their girls in the charge of Mrs. Temple, a woman in charge of women. Later, after dinner, they would join up again and then there would be dancing and flirtation as usual, when they had all had their baths and changed their clothes and got themselves into the evening mood.

Meanwhile they were all dusty and tired and excited. Over-excited. Mr. Dale could not hear what the college girls were saying to Mrs. Temple. What they were saying evidently counted for little; she was observing them with an eye that skidded away from the ear. He was amused by the difference between her manner towards them and their manner towards her. They were still under the excitement of their descent into the chasm; she, who had not ridden down with them, was cool; richer than they by some experience not gained solely by a descent a mile deep into the earth. A mile deep into the earth was nothing to her whose fifty years deep into life must count for something, as life goes.

Mrs. Temple, he judged, must be quite half a century old.

He watched the college girls getting stiffly off their mules; they chattered round her, very young. She listened to them all seriously, making remarks where remarks were needed as though, youthfully eager and uncertain of themselves beneath their self-sufficiency and scorn, they divined in her someone having something to give them, some value to impart; so that, although so manifestly a being from an order other than their own, they could still without apology or mockery divert a portion of their time on their gay progress and consecrate it to her, not for *her* pleasure indeed, in a courteous gesture of youth towards an older person, but for their own pleasure, as a right presumed by the arrogance of their unlicked egoism. Lester Dale, bored man, amused himself by speculating on Mrs. Temple's probable attitude towards them. She must be well aware that nothing but their own inclinations dictated their own actions. At the first moment of boredom or at the first hint of something more inviting, they would have risen like the flock of birds to which she must compare them; risen, as from an exhausted feeding-ground, a field from which the last grains of profit had been pecked, scattering in their inconsequent way on their flight towards the new attraction. But until such a diversion should present itself, she certainly held some kind of appeal for them in their idle moments; some kind of appeal not easy to analyse, since what gift could she bestow on them, he wondered? They could not prize such wisdom and experience as she might be able to share out, for their own experience was—and rightly— dearer to them than any second-hand tested knowledge; perhaps it was because, in their easy way, they knew that she would not sit in critical judgment; would merely enjoy them, amused, older; perhaps also because in no sense could she be regarded as a competitor. They might touch briefly; but never, never could her life threaten an infringement on theirs.

They seemed to take it for granted that she would welcome their company whenever they felt inclined to accord it. No matter if she sat reading a book after dinner; the book that during dinner at her solitary table she had kept propped open by a fork; they arrived like a lot of puppies, and, throwing themselves down on the floor beside her chair, engaged her attention without a thought of being importunate. He had already observed this evening comedy. She lays down her book with a smile. They are right, he thought: this boisterous, arrogant arrival of the group cannot fail to flatter her, though she keeps her sense of flattery always in the right proportion. Their physical presence is in itself a source of pleasure to her. She loves their soft loose limbs and soft warm faces, though I can't decide whether she prefers them in the daytime, in their bright woollen sweaters and bright caps, or in the evening when they have changed into their silks for dinner. In the evening she can see their glossy heads, glossy not only with health but with the constant care of the hairdresser—but far from censuring them for their vanity she must surely commend them for the care of their persons, seeing the ripples of light on the brown, the black, and the fair waves; she must admire the poise of the head on the young shoulders, and the quick turn, the quick toss, the impatience, all the pretty movement, for she is surely hedonistic enough to be grateful for physical beauty even when she cannot match it with mental.

All these things he had noted with detached interest for the past fortnight while he ate his dinner at a table as solitary as Mrs. Temple's; now, seeing her for the first time as a real person, he languidly decided to increase their slight acquaintance. There was an hour to be put away before sunset and he thought he might spend it in her company if she would have him. At the first hint of disinclination on her part he would make an excuse and leave her. He had sufficient regard for his own independence to respect the independence of other people.

He had already decided not to mention the Indian boy. That interview must represent something very private. He would not allude to that. Already he had begun to feel that he should not have I-spied it.

She was standing, looking at the canyon in the evening light. He approached her, conventionally raising his hat.

"Lovely evening, Mrs. Temple."

He instantly disliked himself for saying it and hoped only that she did not dislike him as much as he disliked himself.

> "You came and quacked beside me in the wood,
> You said, It's nice to be alone a bit.
> You said, The sunset's pretty, isn't it?
> By God! I wish, I wish that you were dead!"

As these lines occurred to him, he hoped that they would not occur to her also.

They evidently hadn't, judging by the smile with which she received him. She was either a polite humbug or was really pleased to welcome him. By that smile she had managed to make him feel not unwanted. He knew himself to be a fat squat man, unattractive to women, therefore he was grateful for her courtesy. Kind woman, clever woman! Experience had taught him to distrust woman's wiles, but somehow he could not believe that Helen Temple ever practised woman's wiles; she had no need to do so. Here was a woman with whom he could talk with no nonsense of sex or chivalry; a woman with whom he could meet on equal terms; a woman who was likely to get bored with him as quickly as he was likely to get bored with her; a woman, in short, with whom he could link a brief contact as easily as with another man.

"I can't imagine," he said, "how you manage to put up with all those chattering children. Your patience amazes me—especially with the girls. Minxes not sphinxes —donkeys and monkeys. They cluster round you, but don't they bore you to death?"

He was glad that he had started to talk to her in this real way. He hoped she would respond in equal terms.

She did. Their ideas met.

"No, they don't bore or bother me," she said. "They interest me. I like knowing something about them, and making up stories about their backgrounds. I like knowing about people," she said, cutting her sentence short to stare along the rift of the canyon at that moment of the sinking sun. The sun was still strong though slanting over the desert, but the shadows it cast were deep and fantastic, building the mountains of the canyon into temples and pyramids strongly shadowed with emerging peaks of light.

"No," said Mrs. Temple, after they had both looked for

B

a while, "you make a mistake in thinking that I could ever allow myself to get bored by those children or by anyone here."

"Well," he said, liking her more, "do tell me please what interest enables you to bear the gabble of those children, boys and girls whom you met at the head of the trail just now?"

She looked at him with a new curiosity, seeing him for the first time. She saw a very unattractive man, pallid, pasty, rather too fat; lonely.

She put down her sunshade as the sun was no longer hot enough to make it necessary.

"Let's sit down," she said.

"I am not detaining you?"

"You are not detaining me."

How punctilious he is, she thought.

How gravely well-mannered she is, he thought.

They sat down on a bench. He was grateful to her for not making any comment on the canyon, which was approaching the peak of its sunset magnificence, and she was equally grateful to him.

"So you wonder why I take an interest in my young friends, do you?" she said at last, feeling that if this conversation were going to begin it had better begin quickly. She almost trusted him not to remark on the canyon, but not quite. Not yet.

He was glad she had spoken. He almost trusted her not to remark on the canyon, but not quite. Not yet.

"They all seem to me to be cut very much on a pattern," he began. "Of course I can't tell. You may know them or some of them at home; otherwise, your kindness towards them must be purely impersonal."

"It is, it is," said Mrs. Temple earnestly, "if you can call it kindness. I had never set eyes on any of them before I came here. Naturally I prefer some of them to the others. One of them, for instance, always seems to stand a little apart. I don't know if you will understand me if I say that she seems one of those people for whom a terrible fate is in store. There are people who give one that impression, you know, irrespective of their youth or innocence. Now you will probably set me down as one of those tiresome women who believe themselves to be occult, but I assure you that I am nothing of the sort. I do not have 'feelings,' I do not believe in numerology, or the prophecy of the Pyramids, nor do I tell fortunes by tea-leaves or endeavour to interpret dreams. So don't misjudge me. I am purely matter of fact, but I cannot look at that child without becoming conscious of some very anxious desire to protect her, yet knowing that neither I nor anybody else is capable of doing so."

"I won't ask you what that terrible fate is likely to be, for I am sure you have no idea. You mean, simply, that although the child may be quite commonplace in herself, no different from any other girl of her age though possibly a little more vulnerable, something is coming to her which she cannot escape."

"Thank you for understanding," said Mrs. Temple. "Vulnerable, yes, that is the right word. Mind, this is all mere speculation on my part. I have no inside information. I know nothing whatever about Loraine Driscoll, save that her home is in Massachusetts. I can imagine it pretty clearly and can create a picture of her parents. . . ."

"Please create it for me."

Mrs. Temple changed; she had been speaking seriously, now her eyes twinkled.

"I think I can do that for you if you really want me to. They are an elderly couple, for Loraine is the child of their later years, and her brother is ten years older than herself. They are decent people—so decent that one wonders how they ever brought themselves to commit the grotesque act necessary to beget children. They live in a neat New England town, in a white clap-boarded house

with green shutters, set back a few yards from the main
road which runs through the village under an avenue of
elms. Rather pretty, in a smug way; pleasant enough in
summer, when the trees are green and shady. In winter
bleak and bare; the roads muddy underfoot, and for
months on end there may be snow upon the ground. But
such seasonal severity is a good corrective for the character. The Driscolls' house resembles all the other houses
set along that road. They would not like it to differ in
any way. They have lived in it for thirty years and are
satisfied with it, though I would not say that they have
ever thought about it otherwise than as a convenient and
suitable residence. It stands exposed to the glances of
passers-by on the road, and to the gaze of their neighbours
on either side, but it has never occurred to the Driscolls
any more than it has occurred to anyone else in the village
that privacy might be secured by the planting of a hedge
or the erection of a fence. Such things are not done, nor
have the Driscolls any wish to do them. Life is pure and
open and democratic, so pure as to be almost meaningless,
so democratic as to be almost communal; so pure and open
that neither the Driscolls nor their neighbours trouble to
draw their curtains when evening falls and the lights are
lit. Any evening you may see them sitting there, under
the lamp with the pink shade, Mr. Driscoll reading the
evening paper, Mrs. Driscoll knitting.—Shall I go on?"

"Please go on."

"Mr. Driscoll is a spare man with a brown bony face
and grey hair. He wears rimless glasses, cut square. Not
a harsh man,—he can rub the dog behind its ears in
quite a kindly way,—obviously a man of the utmost
rectitude and probity. In business, of course, he would
not hesitate to get the better of a weaker rival, would not
hesitate to take advantage of someone else's mistake, but
in no way would he consider this a departure from the
high moral standards of his private life. Possibly this is

because he has never thought about it; possibly because in business, as in private life, he accepts other people's standards as he finds them, ready-made. He holds certain views which admit of no argument or modification, but those, again, have been transmitted to him; he has not worked them out for himself. In this, as in everything else, he and Mrs. Driscoll are in perfect tacit harmony. Tacit, because their reserve and decency shun any discussion or examination of things which are better taken for granted. Such examination would be unnecessary and distressing, and the thing they dread most in life is any crisis involving exposure. Safety and orderliness is the rule which they have agreed to maintain. Firmly, quietly, they have achieved their ideal. Rather grimly, perhaps, but if it satisfies them let us wish for both their sakes that nothing ever happens to disturb it."

"Very benevolent of you. I suspect it is only because you believe them to be incorrigible,—no good upsetting them, you know,—and also because you are not really interested."

"On the contrary, having plenty of leisure and nothing better to do I am very much interested. I like thinking about the Driscolls. I like thinking about any family— strange little unit. I like thinking about them in their little box of a house, so exposed in one sense, so isolated in another. The parents, and then the children, so closely held at first, but getting ready all the time to break off into little separate pieces on their own."

"Tell me more about Mrs. Driscoll."

"Surely you know Mrs. Driscoll already? If not, I have done my sketch very badly. She is about five years younger than her husband, somewhere between fifty and fifty-five, rather short and plump and busy, white hair very beautifully waved; she wears a brooch with a miniature of her son as a little boy. If you admire it, she will take it off and turning it over will show you how

fair the lock of his hair was then, although it is now so
dark, an alteration she appears to consider remarkable,
if not unique. The son is her heart's joy and pride; you
have seen him here for yourself, Robert Driscoll, handsome beyond reason; he ought to be a film star instead of
a pilot in the Air Force. I dislike him myself extremely
though I am sure his mother prefers him to poor Loraine.
But I was telling you about his mother, wasn't I? and not
about that offensively handsome young man. She has a
certain voluble animation and ready laughter which
make her husband glance tenderly at her, and lead one
to suspect that this is what attracted him to her when
they were both young, added to his intention of settling
down in marriage with a girl of approved family. This
animation and energy render Mrs. Driscoll a valuable as
well as a respected member of the community. Indeed,
the local Women's Club does not know how it would get
on without her. Mrs. Driscoll would not be happy without
plenty of occupation, so apart from ordering her own
house most efficiently she really orders the entire village.
She likes to wake every morning with the knowledge that
she has a full day before her. She goes to her desk and
consults her engagement- block with satisfaction. Only on
Saturday evenings does she allow herself some relaxation,
when she reads a novel instead of knitting between dinner
and bed. She has approved authors who never disturb or
disappoint, for their values are similar to her own,
morally, sentimentally, and in their rules of conduct;
never an unorthodox suggestion or uncomfortable idea.
The same is true of her friends. She has friends, you must
know, who all admire her greatly,—'A really fine woman,
Mrs. Driscoll,' though I wonder if they could say very
precisely in what her fineness consists, except for the
certainty that she would instantly dismiss a servant-girl
who bore a child in love and not in wedlock. The Driscolls
entertain their friends to dinner once a week, and once

a week they go out to dinner at one house or another, like
Visiting Partners in the old dance: Bow, curtsey, waltz,
take hands, revolve in a circle, return to place, bow.
I suppose that they get some pleasure out of these enter-
tainments, though more likely it is the reassuring habit
of solidarity which chases them out to dinner under rain
or snow in mufflers and overshoes. And although they
call themselves friends, and would tell you that they have
visited pleasantly for the last twenty-five years or more,
I doubt whether their conversation or their current of
feeling has ever gone deeper below the surface than the
works of Mrs. Driscoll's favourite authors. No electric
moments, leaping like sparks on a frosty night! Decorum
will blanket the electric moments, the dangerous moments,
and as for conversation there are so many topics, not so
much inexhaustible as recurrent—politics for the men,
local affairs and gossip of one kind and another for the
women. In principle Mrs. Driscoll disapproves of gossip,
and would tell you that she always discourages it, but in
practice nothing can happen in the village without
reaching her ears and incurring her judgement. Curiously
enough, she is equally interested in tales of the great and
famous whom she has never known and is never likely
to know, but here she does not censure: she merely
marvels. Hollywood and the princes of Europe may do
as they please, and the more extravagant their personal
behaviour the better Mrs. Driscoll likes it."

"Her husband, I imagine, does not share this taste?"

"On the contrary, the patience with which he listens
to her is really a concealed pleasure. Not only does he
like to feel superior to a woman's weakness, but although
he would never admit it he also enjoys a vicarious titil-
lation through the recital of other people's follies. Especially when they are follies which are never likely to touch
his own household.—There is an eagle flying above our
heads," said Mrs. Temple without looking up.

"How did you know?"

She showed him the outstretched shadow stationary upon the desert. The lowering sun distorted it, making it twice its natural size.

"I should feel sorry for the Driscolls," she went on, "if such a shadow ever fell across their lawn. I believe you are right about not wanting to upset them. Only a very *mauvais esprit* wants to startle people whom it is hopeless to change. It would be no more amusing than bursting a paper bag behind their ears. Only, perhaps, for the sake of someone else might one wish to sacrifice them."

"?"

"Well, they have two children, as you know. The young man will take care of himself, only too well. Mr. Driscoll will lend Mrs. Driscoll his handkerchief to dry her tears and will murmur something about boys being boys, trying to keep the chuckle out of his voice. Robert will be forgiven all his errors. His parents will even turn them into a source of pride, saying that all healthy young men ought to be like that. They will not see that Robert has nothing to recommend him except his good looks, which are no merit of his. They will not see that he is as cheap as the daily newspaper. But I do wonder what will happen to Loraine. Perhaps I exaggerate my dread on her behalf. Fortunately for her she is no rebel by nature, so perhaps she will be quite content to marry in the ordinary way and continue to accept her mother's advice in everything. Mrs. Driscoll will remark that instead of losing a daughter she has gained another son and will forget all the anxieties she has already endured on Loraine's account."

"But what anxieties can that docile child already have given her?"

"Educational so far, not personal. Mrs. Driscoll discovered that all Loraine's friends were going to college and that discovery gave her food for very serious thought.

Mrs. Driscoll does not approve of colleges for women, yet if Mrs. Ephraim P. Heffer and Mrs. Cyrus J. Hinks can send their daughters to Vassar or Wellesley, there seemed no valid reason why Mrs. Driscoll should not do likewise, especially in face of Loraine's own rather wistful desire. Besides she is more than a little afraid of Mrs. Heffer's and Mrs. Hinks' criticism; she does not mind being thought old-fashioned, which gives a certain distinction, but she cannot endure to be thought economical."

Mr. Dale laughed politely. Mrs. Temple amused him. He liked her thumb-nail sketch and thought that there was something in her voice which made her words sound less shallow than they might appear if they were written down. There was something in her voice which deepened her words beyond the chatter of a witty woman trying to entertain and possibly attract a bored man. There was a mixture of humanity, tolerance and apartness which pleased him.

"Are you a novelist?" he asked her.

He had never known a novelist but had heard of their cynical ways and became suddenly suspicious lest a woman he liked might be using life in the hotel as Copy. Her portrait of the Driscolls suggested all too glibly the setting provided for the accomplished novelist for a family tragedy. He was relieved when she frankly laughed.

"No, I'm not a novelist," she said. "Sink your suspicions into a grave. I've never written a word of fiction in my life and am not likely to begin now. In spite of that, or perhaps because of that, I am a punctual woman. Do you not think that we should now return to the hotel in time for dinner? I like to have a little time to myself before dinner and I expect you do, too. So shall we go?" she said, rising, and floating away along the path.

He accompanied her, not feeling at all that he had been dismissed but merely that she had brought their conversation to an end at the exact point where it demanded to be brought to an end. As they walked together towards the hotel he wondered whether he ought to fill up the gap in their talk by asking her some topical question as "Do you know when the manœuvres are due to take place?"

He took no real interest in the manœuvres and it was apparent from the vagueness of her reply that she took no interest in them either. To-morrow, she thought, or perhaps next week: she wasn't sure. They pursued their path in a comfortable silence.

§

Mrs. Temple gained the solitude of her own room, but was not long allowed to enjoy it. A knock at her door roused her. She saw Loraine Driscoll carrying a sheaf of poinsettias.

"I thought maybe you would wear one of these, Mrs. Temple." She glanced round the room, discovering a white dress laid out on the bed. "On your white dress," she added, associating the white and the red with her vision.

The child was shy; she laid the flowers on the bed humbly, as one who begs not to be repulsed. She gave Mrs. Temple a soft sideways look; I know I should not have followed you to your room, but let me in, admit me, let me stay.

Again that look as of an unfinished drawing in the soft contours and limpid eyes. The unwritten page. She lingered; there was an uneasiness somewhere; she fingered the silver on the dressing-table; touched the high-lights with the tip of her finger, as though it were a game she absently played, thinking of something else as she played it.

The room was quiet and cool, the windows bare to the sunset. So Mrs. Temple lets the last rays into her room, does she, unwilling to lose one last moment of beauty? Does she also let in the moonlight, leaning at her window for a last look down into the canyon, transformed by that strange illumination into the colourless semblance of a landscape which might be on the moon itself? Might I perhaps one night join her at her window in silence, creeping away as the moon sinks without a word spoken?

Mrs. Temple meanwhile, having recovered herself from her annoyance at the intrusion, discovered with amusement her own surprise at seeing one of the gang away from the others. So accustomed was she to accepting them as a band, a gang, that she could with difficulty accommodate herself to the idea of their separate existence. Yet, as she had told Mr. Dale, Loraine had always seemed apart, tenderer than the others, trailed in their wake, tolerated, but more secretive, as though she had a more particularized life than they with their freemasonry and their air of initiation to things of which they could know little.

She wants to talk to me; she is in distress; she wants to tell me something.

"Wait a moment," she said to gain time, and taking up her dress she went into the bathroom next door. Loraine waited, looking at everything. Mrs. Temple returned, all in sleek ivory now and fastened a flower against her shoulder, bending forward to see it in the mirror under the light. The red of the flower struck like fresh blood. Loraine watched her, one woman watching another adorn herself.

"What a grand flower, Loraine. How kind of you. But where did you find them? They don't grow here, they're not indigenous. Not even at the bottom of the canyon."

"They came up from Mexico," said Loraine. "There was a man with a big basket, selling them in the hall as we came in."

All this seemed irrelevant, and now that her thanks had

been expressed Mrs. Temple hoped that the girl would go. The girl showed no signs of going, but lingered by the dressing-table with the touching lack of *savoir-faire* of the young. In this again she differed from her companions who gave the impression of being able to deal with any social situation. It became necessary to make some further remark.

"Have you had a nice day, Loraine?"

"You met us coming back. We went riding."

"That was nice."

"I didn't much want to go."

How easy to ask why not. What was the sudden obstinacy which prevented one from saying the thing one was intended to say? Perhaps merely because she shrank from inviting a confidence. She noticed that Loraine avoided saying where they had been: that might mean nothing or everything. Mrs. Temple had acquired the habit of noticing such things. But for the moment she was intent only on dismissing Loraine as gently as possible.

"Well, you have been more than thoughtful in bringing me these superb flowers. I suppose you should go down to dinner now? Your friends will blame me if you keep them waiting. Your nice Miss Carlisle may even be cross."

She will shut me out of her room, she will exclude me. Perhaps she is even angry at my having crept in. She does not know I came because I was afraid. Yet how could she not know? she is grown-up, she knows everything. I am here now; I shall perhaps never be here again. I will force myself to speak.

"Mrs. Temple."

"Yes?"

"What would one do,—what do people do, I mean,— if something terrible were to happen? Would one find courage for it, anywhere?"

"What put that into your head? Are you worried about anything?"

I can't tell her, now that she asks; I can't.

"Oh no, Mrs. Temple; I just wondered."

"I expect one finds courage, somewhere," said Helen, looking at her.

"Some people do, perhaps; not all. Surely it depends on how one is made? Surely some people find it very difficult to resist?"

"To resist the something terrible?"

"No, to resist other people. To resist getting crushed."

"To know what one really wants, do you mean, Loraine? If one had to take an important decision?"

Is it possible that the child wants to adopt a profession and that her parents want to oppose it? Stiff Puritanical folks; quite likely.

"No, not exactly. Sometimes people make terrible mistakes, don't they, Mrs. Temple? Mistakes they can't undo?"

"It does happen," said Helen, smiling. But she felt lazy, unwilling to make the effort to meet this innocent perplexity. Perhaps a little unkindness, too, prompted her to thwart the confidence. Unexpected unkindnesses rose up, sometimes, in the kindest hearts. An unaccountable reluctance to take responsibility, or an unrealized desire for power? Power over another being, however young, however vulnerable? She knew that if she withheld her advice now, Loraine would return to seek it again.

"It does happen," said Helen; "but I am sure you would never make such a mistake, Loraine. You strike me as a very well-balanced young woman." How untrue! "That's what strikes me most about all American girls," she continued, trying to generalize; "you do know how to manage your own lives, far better than our English girls ever did, while they had the chance. You seem to grow up at an earlier age, thus losing less time in attaining maturity." What nonsense I am talking, I don't believe a word of all this. Americans never grow up at all, they remain permanently adolescent, that's their charm if they only knew it, though they don't like being told so. They pretend to be adult, but it will take them centuries before they become as adult as Europe. They are neither war-worn nor out-worn and that makes the whole difference. I hope they may escape being war-worn for some centuries, and as for being out-worn they have centuries ahead of them before one can possibly begin to use the word decadent. It will take them centuries to become out-worn; I prefer that word to decadent. Dear me, she thought, what platitudes! but my observation of America makes them true, and meanwhile I must go on talking to this poor child who is waiting for my answer. "Dear Loraine," she said, "don't worry overmuch. One always has problems to meet and believe me one always meets them as they come. If ever I can really help you, I hope you'll let me try. But you know it is very difficult to help another person. I'll do my best. Now don't you think you ought to go down to dinner?"

Dinner! Dinner! It sounded like a dog being coaxed to its meal. Mrs. Temple felt the implication. It was the phrase by which, tactfully and recently, she had disposed of Mr. Dale. It now became the phrase by which she hoped to dispose of Loraine. She had been very careful not to sit down while talking to Loraine, since when one sits down it makes one's uprising more marked when one wishes to dismiss a guest. She had wandered about the room, taking things up and setting things down as she moved. It was thus easy for her to stray towards the door; open it politely; shoo Loraine out on to the corridor; and close the door behind her.

She closed it gently, not to hurt the child's feelings. She closed it firmly, to be sure that the child wouldn't come back. Click went the catch; the child was now safely pushed out onto the corridor. She must now be on her way down to dinner.

§

The corridor was deserted as Loraine came out of Mrs. Temple's room. Mrs. Temple had shut the door so quietly behind her that Loraine stood for a moment, aware of the stillness and of the depth of the pile carpet under her feet. Why was it that just when one felt most frightened and forlorn, one gained such extraordinary consciousness of inanimate objects, as though they stood in a life of their own, mute and very static? Were they friendly or hostile? Certainly they were not indifferent; they watched with some sort of an eye. The only question was whether that eye was friendly or baleful.

She wished she were back in Mrs. Temple's room. The grace of the older woman gave her comfort. Mrs. Temple's possessions seemed to share her gracefulness. The silver looked so serene, and some of the highlights had been pink and amethyst where the sunset reflected in them. Loraine wished she could stay and bathe for an hour in that assurance; she would not have asked to be allowed to talk, only to sit and heal.

Voices came up from below. She began slowly to descend the stairs.

On the landing a door opened and someone looked out. Loraine knew her, it was Madame de Retz, the Polish woman. She felt instantly that Madame de Retz spent quite a lot of time behind that door waiting for someone to pass so that she might creep out on them.

"Ah, Miss Driscoll, my dear. So you are back from your ride? And changed already! Won't you come in for a little chat? I show you my Grigori, he has learnt some new words."

"That's kind of you, madame, thank you so much, but I think perhaps I ought to go down to dinner."

"The bell has not yet sounded," said Madame de Retz inexorably.

She made Loraine precede her into the room. Unlike
Mrs. Temple's room, it was darkened, the curtains were
drawn, the sunset excluded; only one pink lamp stood
beside the divan, and it was hot, airless, secretive.

Madame de Retz sank on to the divan and patted it for
Loraine to sit near her.

"Now come and tell me all you have been doing. You
young people, what a good time you have, riding, dancing,
playing, perhaps flirting. Those handsome boys! but none
so handsome as your brother. Ah, if I were twenty years
younger how your brother would attract me!"

The parrot gave a sudden inhuman shriek, and flying
up to the picture-rail he perched there, eyeing Loraine
with his head on one side.

"Grigori, you naughty boy, you quite startled Miss
Driscoll. Come here at once and tell her how clever you
become."

Madame de Retz held out her hand, clicking her
fingers towards the bird, which flew down and settled
on her shoulder. He was a beautiful jade-green little bird,
with a plum-coloured necklet and a wicked red eye.
Loraine noticed the brilliance of his plumage against the
square black hair and sallow complexion of his mistress.
He nibbled at her ear as though he were telling her a
secret.

"I bring him from India," said Madame de Retz. "Is
he not exquisite, so neat, so sleek, so well-groomed? He
loves fruit and jewels, and if I mislay a ring I know where
to look for it. Now Grigori, you tell Miss Driscoll where
she has been to-day."

Grigori, unwilling to speak, hopped down on to a bowl
of fruit, and in the harsh squeak of a marionette uttered
the words, "Bright Angel Trail."

Loraine found it extremely disagreeable that Madame
de Retz and even her bird should know what she had
been doing. It suggested an interest in other people's

affairs which displeased and disquieted her. Now Mrs.
Temple had either not known or not cared; all she had
done was to enquire casually if Loraine had had a nice
day.

"How does he know?" said Loraine trying to be polite.

"One has eyes, one has ears, one has windows," cried
Madame de Retz mischievously. "But it is for the young,
Bright Angel Trail. It is too dangerous for the old, those
precipices, those sliding stones, those changes of climate,
those legends which tell that anything might happen there.
We older people are safer to remain on the Rim. But for
the young it is good to have adventures, all kinds of
adventures. Perhaps you have already been told that by
your friend the so charming Mrs. Temple?"

"I'm afraid I can't claim Mrs. Temple as my friend,"
said Loraine; "I scarcely know her. She is very kind to
all of us, but I doubt if she knows one of us from the
other."

"At any rate, she calls *you* by your Christian name,"
said Madame de Retz in her shrewd way. "Of course,"
she added as an after-thought, "your parents are very
rich?"

"Not very," said Loraine. She had heard people say
that her father was a millionaire but she never believed
such rumours on hearsay. "Not very rich," she said, and
then stopped because she felt that Madame de Retz was
trying to get information.

The parrot shrieked again, suddenly as before. He was
holding a peach in his claw, tearing wounds with his beak
in its flesh. He and the peach looked very decorative
together. Between each stab of attack he looked up and
shrieked.

"Gri-gor-i!" said Madame de Retz in the indulgent
reproachful tone of an unwise mother. "Do not scream
like that. You startle my guest. Say your word nicely,
your new words. Speak, Grigori, my little boy," and she

added some words which Loraine recognized as Polish but could not understand. "Speak, Grigori, my little boy," and added some other words in a language Loraine could not identify. "You see," said Madame de Retz with a little laugh, "I tell him in Hindustani. I tell him to speak his new words. I tell him now in English: Grigori, speak your new words. You see, he will obey."

"Bright Angel Trail," screamed the bird, and plunged its beak into the soft peach again.

"You are white, my dear," said Madame de Retz; "you have grown pale. Does my Grigori frighten you, with his Bright Angel Trail? What a silly bird he is, and what a silly woman I am to let you be frightened by a bird just when you were on your way to dinner. Too bad! Shall we go down to dinner together now we have been having this little interlude? But no," she added as an after-thought, "you have told me nothing about you yet. Stop for a little more. This is an intimate hour, isn't it? You must have lots of secrets, my dear, the small intimate secrets of a young girl. Trust me, my dear. I am an old woman in your eyes, but I know how to be a friend to the young. I love humanity, especially young humanity. See," she said, pointing to a row of ledgers standing in a book-case, "that is all to do with humanity, all which is written in those big books."

"You have managed to arrange your room very nicely," said Loraine, who did not wish to talk about herself. "It does not look like an hotel room at all."

"You think so? Ah, if you were a poor lonely woman like me, with no home, moving from hotel to hotel, you would also make your room not like an hotel room. I take my poor possessions with me, and in every place I go to I say to the proprietor please may I set up my divan, my cushions, my bits of silk on the walls, and may I get my bookshelves made to take my books, to make my room like home."

"But you haven't many books, madame," said Loraine looking round; "only those two shelves full of ledgers that look like a counting-house."

"Ah, you mean I am not a great reader," cried Madame de Retz with her shrill laugh that reminded Loraine of the parrot's scream. "What a clever child, to put her finger on my weakness. No, I cannot read. Life fascinates me, not books. That is why I say my ledgers as you call them contain all humanity. That is why I ask you to tell me about yourself. Love of life, my child, that is what inspires me. Life represented by children like you and your handsome brother. The young generation. Your ambitions, your difficulties, your loves. Of course one does not wish to be indiscreet. The secrets of a young girl, as I said. One does not wish to intrude on them. Yet when one becomes an old woman one hopes to help the young a little. Experience, you know; helpful, perhaps. Of course I know the young disregard it. A little boy said to me once, 'You told me the path was slippery but I never really believed you till I came down crack on my head.'"

Madame de Retz is very friendly, thought Loraine, and very sympathetic. Why is it that I don't like her better and that she frightens me? I don't like her hands, they are too thin, like claws. I don't like her square black hair and her sallow face. I don't like her frowsty room and her horrid beautiful bird. She wants something from me, but what is it? Is she trying to pry into my own life or is it money she wants? She did ask me if my parents were very rich. I don't know if they are or not. I believe they are. I don't think my father is Big Business but I think he is a sort of first cousin to it. He says mysterious things sometimes which sound as though he had something to do with Wall Street. Perhaps he is just trying to impress us at home. Anyhow we have always lived as though there were no need to bother about money. Robert and I have always had everything we wanted, look at Robert's

car, and Mother gets a new string of pearls on our birth-
days. Pearls cost dollars; every pearl is a shining coin. I
wish we had coins instead of dollar-bills. Silver looks real,
paper looks pretence. Silver and gold have a beauty;
paper might be an advertisement you tear up and throw
into the wastepaper basket. Token wealth; yet I suppose
it means something. How odd not to know if your father
is really rich or just half-rich. Why do parents conceal
such things from their children? Why is there always such
secrecy about money? Either people boast or else they
conceal; they don't seem ever to get it right. If I had
money, or if I hadn't money, if I were rich or if I were
poor, I wouldn't mind anybody knowing about it one
way or the other. I just don't understand the pretence
that goes on about it either way. It doesn't seem to matter.
If some people have too much money they should share
it out with people who haven't enough; that's how I see
it. Robert says so, too, but although he talks far better
than I do I don't believe he means half of what he says.
He is like our father, with a difference. Neither of them
says what he means. I would like to say what I mean but
something stops me. Just now, I couldn't tell Mrs. Temple
anything of what I really meant. How could I? It was
mad of me to think I could. I hoped she would guess and
help me. She didn't guess, or did she? I don't know. I
wish she could guess and help. I like her. I don't like
Madame de Retz. Madame de Retz is much more
friendly towards me than Mrs. Temple is; I think that is
because Madame de Retz is curious to discover whether
my father is very rich or not; Mrs. Temple wouldn't care.
Madame de Retz is talking now; I haven't been listening;
I don't know what she has been saying. She is asking me
if I need pocket-money. She is not trying to get money
from me, she is offering me money instead. How surprising! What is she saying?

"You have a princess at your college, yes, no? Not a

real princess, of course, not a Royal Highness or Imperial, but *still* a princess. A Balkan princess! Poor but pretty. She has a complexion she could sell to American ladies for thousands of dollars, if one could sell one's complexion." The parrot squawked as he speared a cherry with his beak. He held it up in his claw and pecked at it delicately. It matched his red beak and his red eye. He held it up, aware of his decorative value, pecking once and then looking round for approval. He pecked again, a quick, sharp, vicious peck. He was right in his estimation of himself: he and the cherry made a beautiful composition. Design and colour blended into perfection. "Grigori!" Madame de Retz said lovingly, and then returned to her theme about the complexion of the Balkan princess.

She means Irma, thought Loraine. A dull girl whose only merit is the complexion Madame de Retz refers to and her title. Those are the things that have value in the eyes of Madame de Retz. Those are the things that have value in the eyes of everybody here; in the eyes of everybody I know. Mrs. Temple is the only exception. Mrs. Temple doesn't give a damn for complexions or titles. I don't know what Mrs. Temple does give a damn for, but it certainly isn't for anything that appeals to Madame de Retz.

"You are friends, yes, you and Princess Irma? You have the intimacy of young girls? The hair-brushing, the bedroom confidences? Ah, the grace of those hours! The ease of the négligé, the little bare toes wriggling inside soft slippers, the shaded lights, the bed turned down, the clock ticking on telling you to go to bed, but you don' go to bed, for there is always something more to say! But one thing is lacking in these days: the firelight. Now, when I was a girl in Poland we had beautiful fires of wood that were real fires, not like these electric fires which are cold although they are hot; you could poke our fires and make a fresh flame and then our talk made a fresh flame too. There were my cousins and I, all girls together when the boys were away; girls together like you and the Princess Irma, so close in the freemasonry of all the little secrets."

"I think electric fires are very nice," said Loraine. "So little trouble, so convenient."

"Bad girl, you try to—what is it?—put me off. But I am interested in your friend. So sad, I think, these exiles. No throne, no Court, no country, no money. Wanderers. She shall find it very difficult, poor Irma, to be among you American girls all so rich. Now would you like to do your friend a good turn if I tell you how?"

"She isn't a friend of mine, madame, really she isn't. Not a particular friend."

"Bad girl again, first you say Mrs. Temple is not a friend and now Irma. Soon you will tell me you have no friends in the world. But even if she is not a friend, not a particular friend, you would like to do a poor college-mate a good turn. Ah, I see you look curious. You wonder, do you not, how this lonely stranger can help to benefit your princess. Well, the secret lies in those big books. Come, shall I show you?"

"Another time, perhaps, madame," said Loraine, who now thought that Madame de Retz must be mad, "but you must excuse me now, I hear the bell ringing and Miss Carlisle does not like us to be late for dinner."

"Ah, yes, your Miss Carlisle," said Madame de Retz who knew when it was inopportune to insist. "Of course she has charge of all you young ladies and must keep discipline. She does not look like the principal of a college, ("She isn't the principal," began Loraine, but was waved aside,) but she knows her duty. Shall I tell you what her duty is? It is first to see that you do not get into trouble and then to see that you do get into marriage."

"Into marriage?" said Loraine, really surprised.

Madame de Retz gave her shrill laugh, faithfully echoed by Grigori. She was so much pleased with the success of her remark that she reached forward and patted Loraine's knee.

"Dear child, do you think all your parents send you here for what you call fun? This little happy holiday-party to the Grand Canyon, a treat? All those nice college boys are here of course by collaboration ("Our college happens to be co-ed," said Loraine stoutly), and all those young officers, the airmen, the lieutenants, the young captains, is it coincidence that you come where they are assembled? Have you not all already your flirts, your beaux amongst them?"

"Do you know, madame, I don't believe American boys and girls think that way so much as perhaps you Europeans do. You see, we are used to growing up together."

"Pooh," said Madame de Retz. "You shuffle, (she pronounced it sherffle) you pretend. All boys and girls think that way. Americans, Europeans, and Chinese. It is just all this necking and petting makes you believe different. At the back may not be Love in your minds, but always Marriage in the mind of your parents. An arm round the neck may lead to a ring round the finger."

"I really must go, madame," said Loraine, getting up. "Go then, go then," said Madame de Retz in a soothing voice, "and you will come back, yes? Or, look, I open the door again just as you come down the stairs and call you for another little talk? That will be nice. Go now, find your friends and your Miss Carlisle at your merry table, and I wave to you across the saloon from my lonely table. I wave to you with the smile of understanding, you return the smile and that is enough: we are friends, n'est ce pas?"

She smiled bravely and brightly now, the smile of a

martyr. Loraine escaped, but not without a sense of guilt.
Had she been sympathetic enough? Had she misjudged
Madame de Retz?

§

The dining-saloon filled up with people and chatter as
the hour for feeding approached. The animals must
be fed. Animals in the Grand Canyon Zoo couldn't
be allowed to go hungry. The hotel was doing well;
never since its inception had it enjoyed such a season as
this, when the published announcement of the manœuvres
attracted holiday-makers from all parts of the continent
as well as the faithful habitués and the unusual come-and-
go of soldiers old and young who, bored with living in
tents in the constant company of their mess-mates, sought
distraction by straying into the hotel for cocktails and
then remaining for dinner. The hotel, in fact, scarcely
knew how to cope with all the people wanting to use it.
Its resources were strained; the employés had never
anticipated such a demand; they got flustered, ran about
unnecessarily, lost their heads when visitors strolled up
to the reception bureau asking questions, tried to remain
polite and helpful according to the tradition in which
they had been trained. ("Never let a guest see that you
think him a nuisance; that you are at a loss for a reply;
that you cannot furnish the information required; that
you are tired, irritable, overworked; that there are other
guests who need attention and who are waiting their
turn; remember that guests are always impatient, never
patient; that they all think they pay enough for their
money to buy politeness and immediate competent
service; keep your head, satisfy everyone, be amiable,
helpful, sympathetic; never show that you have any
human feelings or failings at all.") Hard demands were
now made on them; demands which had never been made

on their first engagement. On their first engagement they
had merely been told that they should serve in the Grand
Canyon hotel, an ordinary hotel service in an extraordinary place; but the extraordinary place didn't affect
them, since one hotel was very much the same as another
hotel wherever it was, and they didn't take much notice
of the canyon outside. Taking service in an hotel meant
taking service in an hotel, and that was that. It meant
the usual routine and the usual things one had been
trained to do. Just an hotel, a tiny world sporadically
invaded and inhabited by strangers, come to-day and
gone to-morrow, strangers who had to be treated with
deference, however much one liked or disliked them.
Cooks must cook; waitresses wait; managers manage;
porters be portative; the reception bureau be receptive.
All must be amiable, welcoming, helpful. Merciful Mother
of God, what a task.

The only person who seemed completely unshaken was
the Manager. He seemed to be enjoying himself, a happy
cork bobbing on the waves of this sudden excessive
business. He was here, he was there, he popped up everywhere he was wanted. He bobbed and popped. He was
at the bureau, at the cocktail bar, in the lounge, in the
kitchen. A deft touch, leaving everyone soothed and
satisfied. A man of genius in his own way. He had the
required touch of tact. He soothed the guests, he soothed
the staff, he soothed the central management from New
York whenever they got hold of him over the telephone.
He always knew the right word to say. Whenever his
central management got him on a long-distance call, he
was able to convince them quietly that he was quite able
to deal with the rush of business due to people arriving
at that lone outpost the Grand Canyon Hotel in Arizona
where the forces of the United States were concentrating
for their manœuvres.

The central management was a nuisance to him with

their long-distance calls. Why could they not trust him
to manage things locally for them, without bothering a
man perpetually, interrupting him even while he was
eating his dinner? He was working hard enough for them
from morning to night, and working sideways for his own
purposes too, a full-time job for any man; it was not fair
to interrupt a man sitting down to snatch a mouthful of
mutton at the very moment he expected to have a moment
to himself and to be able to think about a man's personal
life. It was hard to be perpetually on tap; never to be
able to shut himself into his little office behind the bureau
and give orders that he was not to be disturbed. Not even
half an hour to himself for a nap. Always ready to emerge
smiling, when the discreet tap came on his door from
his clerk and a whisper informed him that Mister or
Missis or Miss Blank was waiting to speak to him. Inwardly
hurling the mister, missis, or miss to the bottom of the
canyon, he must emerge bland, urbane. "Now just what
can I do for you, sir, madame?" Be of service; always be
of service. You had a toothache, had you? Pooh. Managers
don't have toothaches.

So he smiled. As he had a squashed-up face, triangular,
rather Mongolian, rather like a cat, he could smile
effectively. His face broadened out sideways as he smiled.
It was not a pleasant smile, for those who could notice; it
suggested that he would knife you in the back for a buck
or even for the sheer pleasure of doing it; but fortunately
for his flock of guests few people did notice. To most of
them he was just a smile poised above a black morning-
coat, with pin-stripe trousers. The Manager was very
particular about the correctness of his clothes. His predecessor had sloped round in corduroy slacks and a khaki
shirt open at the neck; the new manager had altered all
that. He believed in local colour and exploited it freely,
but he also believed in the metropolitan touch for himself
and his reception clerk. They were the only black-coats

in the hotel and he had contrived to persuade the central management that it paid. Let everybody else be as picturesque as you like; let them go about in fancy dress, those dude-ranch boys; encourage them, indeed, to do so; but let the reception bureau suggest the Waldorf-Astoria. He believed in the value of contrast. He was an artist after his own fashion.

That was why he called his clients sir or madame, instead of by their names in the friendly familiar American way. It gave a touch of old London; a touch of old Paris; it startled them, made them notice him. It was deliberate. Everything he did was deliberate.

This time it was Mrs. Temple waiting to speak to him. He did not like Mrs. Temple, knowing that he failed to impress her. He noted, however, that she wore one of his poinsettias pinned against her shoulder. It had been clever of him to arrange for those poinsettias to come up from Mexico; little surprises like that amused the guests, and he usually managed to provide at least one surprise a day. Besides he had been glad of the opportunity to exchange a few quiet words with the man from Mexico. The poinsettias had given him a good excuse.

Mrs. Temple wanted to know if a note awaited her.

The Manager, swirling neatly on his heel, whisked it out of her pigeon-hole and flicked it down on the desk before her with the air of one who deals out the fourth ace. The trim little typed envelope caught his attention, and although Mrs. Temple was not a person at whom one winked he permitted himself a slight raising of the eyebrows accompanied by a slight jerk of the thumb over his shoulder in the direction of the Painted Desert. It all indicated very subtly and respectfully that he and Mrs. Temple might be sharing an innocent secret. Mrs. Temple did not respond. Too much of the English lady, he thought, stung to vexation; too much of the English lady to share a joke however innocent with an American manager. He put down another mark against Mrs. Temple's name. She had snubbed him again.

Still he could not stop himself from admiring what he called her poise as she crossed the lounge on her way towards the dining-saloon. She had a manner about her, that woman; a grand manner. She was different from the other tourists whom he despised.

A cheerful noise was coming from the dining-saloon. In a few moments he must make his appearance there, stopping at each table, bending down to enquire whether everyone was perfectly satisfied. Nothing would have induced him to neglect this piece of routine. But that could wait for a little, until the diners were further under way. He had found by experience that a man is better disposed half way through his dinner than at the beginning of it, and although he was always prepared to rectify complaints he preferred to avoid receiving them. Meanwhile, very well contented with himself, he remained standing behind his bureau, delicately propping himself by the tips of his fingers on the polished surface, swaying slightly on his toes, and permitted himself the luxury of surveying the empty lounge. Quite soon, he knew, his two bell-hops would come running in to their evening task of putting everything tidy, shaking up the cushions, pulling the chairs into position, emptying the ash-trays, taking away the cocktail glasses (and, he suspected, finishing off the dregs as soon as they got out of the room. He must see to that). Their arrival would be the signal for his own progress into the dining-saloon, but such was the precision and severity of his organization that they would not arrive an instant before the appointed hour. He could count on having the lounge to himself for another five minutes. He was pleased with the lounge. It was his creation, a very different affair from the ramshackle hall he had taken over from his predecessor. He had persuaded a sum of money out of the central manage-

ment and had expended it in the furnishings and decora-
tions he judged best suited to the expectation of his
guests. Very full of local colour it was. Navajo blankets
lay on the floor, Mexican serapes were flung carelessly
over the armchairs. (He had hesitated for some time
between these and some very modernistic Fifth Avenue
chintzes.) The effect, he thought, was colourful. Shelves
ranged with Hopi pottery ran round the walls. The wastepaper baskets were of the plaited Papago make. The
mats under the cocktail glasses were Pima make. Similar
objects were purchasable by the souvenir-minded tourist
at the Indian shop opposite, but the tourist was advised
to come to the Manager's office first to be told exactly
how to proceed. He would be invited into the office as a
special favour and in a locked-door condition of secrecy
would be told how very difficult it was to get the Indians
to sell their wares at any price; Indians were queer
people; nobody could understand them unless they had
lived amongst them for years and then not even then;
the queerest things happened amongst Indians; they
twirled sticks to make a noise like falling rain; they used
the yucca fibre to make their baskets; they used the
agave leaves and the reed and a rush which grows by the
Gila River; for their pottery, they used vessels of clay
mixed with cedar bark or corn-husks; they danced
seasonal dances which no white man or woman might
see.

The Manager knew nothing about any of these things,
but he contrived to put up quite a good show of pretence
when his tourists came into his room behind the scenes.
Above all, he knew how to stimulate custom for the shop
opposite. He had become quite glib about the Indians
and their legends. In the very first week of his appointment
he had recognized them as Local Colour. After two years
of his job at the canyon he had learnt how to exploit the
material he had at hand. He exploited it perfectly. He

had mugged up all the necessary information and could now put it across without making a single blunder.

He had taped his clientele.

Leaning his finger-tips on the bureau he wondered whether he might not now ask the central management for a rise of salary.

On the whole he was pleased with life.

The only thing that bothered him, the seed in his tooth, was the uncertainty of the moment when his instructions would arrive. Every time the telephone shrilled, he lifted the receiver in a cold anticipation of hearing the pre-arranged code phrase: "We hope you are finding the new bathroom installation satisfactory," the distant voice would say. "Perfectly satisfactory, O.K." he would have to reply, and then he would replace the receiver and hurry off to set the hotel on fire. His dear hotel, his pet, his creation, his pride, his triumph. He would have to sacrifice it all to the Cause; he would have to see his Local Colour going up into flames. The Manager was a man torn in half. One half of him wanted to advance the Nazi cause; the supreme domination of Germany over the world; the other half wanted to keep his creation intact since he had made it and felt about it as a mother feels about her child; it was his child, and he felt a savage sense of possession; but, committed as he was to the Nazi bribery, he had to destroy the very thing he loved, a hard thing for any man to do, so no wonder that he struck harshly at Sadie when he saw her coming out from the dining-saloon. He vented on her the worry that was in his heart, an oblique relief of ill-temper such as we all indulge in when something else goes wrong.

He did not like Sadie from any point of view; he found her physically repellent with her meagre body unsatisfying to a man of his tastes; he deplored her ill-health, and was irritated by the solicitude she evoked in Mrs. Temple. Sadie was over-worked; Mrs. Temple thought so and

said so. The Manager of course agreed and would see
what could be done about it; then as soon as Mrs. Temple's
back was turned he would invent some unnecessary extra
job for the girl to perform. And now . . .

"Sadie! What you doing here at this time of day?"

She withdrew her handkerchief an inch from her lips
to answer in a whisper, "I'll be down again in a moment."

"Can't hear what you say. Speak up, can't you?"

"You heard me. D'you want to make me cough?"

"Oh, if that's it. . . . Not shamming, are you?"

She silently showed him the handkerchief, stained with
blood.

"Ugh, take it away. And take yourself away, disgracing
the hotel; visitors don't like squalors like you. Come back as
soon as you get yourself presentable again. There'll be a lot
of folk in to-night and plenty to do for all. Be off with you,"
he added sharply, hearing voices and laughter just outside.

§

The diners from the camps were beginning to arrive.
They drifted in through the open door, in little lumps of
twos and threes, laughing and making more noise than
they need. They swaggered a bit, all very manly. Young
officers handing their caps carelessly to the bell-hops;
young airmen very handsome in their slim blue. The
airmen came from the other side of the canyon, from the
North Rim where the aerodrome was. They came in
auto-gyro troop-carrying planes, fluttering down with
twirling blades, settling safely and comfortably from the
air, landing twenty or thirty young men for a good
time for one evening. The planes waited to take them
back; to fly them back over the ten-mile gash of the
canyon. A ten-mile gash meant nothing to a plane flying
at six hundred miles an hour. It meant no more than a
leap taken by a boy with a pole across a brook.

There were a few senior officers, too, and when these came in the young men stepped smartly aside in deference. It all gave an air of life to the place, pleasing the Manager who had once resented being tucked away to run what he considered a one-horse show. In fact, but for a certain bait held out to him, he would never have accepted the job at all.

It was all very bright and cheery now in the hotel. Riding boots tramped on the parquet floor. Presently those boots would be dancing, and the dancing floor outside would be full of masculine boots and feminine slippers moving in rhythm. Several romances had already been observed and the atmosphere after dinner was always love and festivity. This was quite as it should be, with the bright camps outside and the roar of the night-bombers taking off in practice from the other side of the canyon. Daring, Danger, and Dancing,—the Manager thought he might hang that up as a slogan over the cocktail bar. Slogans were always useful. They caught the eye and the mind. They meant nothing. Or did they mean something? Daring, danger. . . . The Manager shrank for himself from either; he preferred to take his risks on the ground, not in the air, secretly in sub-rosa ways, an expression he had picked up in some lecture given somewhere in Brooklyn.

These young men who were coming in to get cocktails or dinner at his hotel gave not a damn for danger or daring. They were not cowards, as the Manager knew himself to be a coward in his morning-coat and pin-stripe trousers. They were full of daring, which he lacked. He hated them for that reason. He loved them for that reason. He was prepared to betray them for that reason.

He had his favourites, and as they passed through the door into the lounge they saluted him cheerfully, calling him by name as a crony. He responded; it was part of his job to respond, so he did it heartily, always keeping that touch of the Waldorf-Astoria, that touch of London, New York, and Paris, in his deferential manner set between himself and his clients. They chaffed him, and he entered into the joke, but always at the back of his vindictive mind was the idea that soon the joke might be on his side. His feelings as he watched them throwing away their money were complex: on the one hand the more they spent the more his pride in his hotel and its receipts was gratified, on the other hand he snarled as he reflected that the price of one man's drinks would cover one week's salary.

It was almost time for him to start on his rounds in the dining-saloon. His reception-clerk had already joined him, ready to take his place, a suppressed youth who acted also as the accountant and who apparently possessed no character at all beyond an astounding facility for adding up figures. But before he could leave his bureau for the saloon the Manager had a decision to take, a decision he had to take every night. Was it warm enough for dancing out of doors?

"Tim."

"Yes, Mr. Royer."

"Take over now. I'm going out to have a look at the night."

"Yes, Mr. Royer."

The same dialogue took place every evening at this hour. It was part of the beautifully organized routine of the hotel. Everything happened on the tick. The bell-hops were there, putting everything straight. Smart little boys they were, well trained. He had dressed them up in Indian clothes to give some additional local colour. Very picturesque they looked, those smart little boys dressed up as little Indians. They didn't look very convincing, since they hadn't the right type of face; but still, they would do, and they carried conviction among the hotel guests and the tourists who knew no better.

D

Anything would do for the tourists who invaded the
hotel or for any of those other people for whom the
Manager had a justified contempt.

They meant nothing more to him than the negro
orchestra which had just arrived. He knew that they
would play throughout dinner and then would go to take
their place out of doors. Three niggers he had there: a
xylophone, a piano, and a trumpet. They would strike up
a gay noise and would keep it up for as long as it was
wanted.

> "I love you, ba-aby,
>   I'll love you as long as can be.
>   I love you, baby,
>   There's only you and me."

He went over to them.
   "Hello, boys."
   "Hello, boss."
   "All fixed up, are you?"
   "All fixed up O.K."
   "Ready to carry on?"
   "O.K. boss, all ready."
   "Carry on then. Strike up."
They struck up, three jolly negroes in white jackets as
white as their teeth. They played incessantly, as though
they really enjoyed playing. They played so well and so
insistently, that the young men in the dining-saloon got
up and asked the girls to dance.

The Manager started on his rounds. He could estimate
the accurate moment when his clients had begun to go
gay. That was the moment when he could safely make
his appearance between the dinner-tables, asking if the
cuisine had been to their liking, and perhaps pressing
another bottle of champagne on those who had already
had enough.

That was the way a skilful manager managed his hotel.

§

After dinner, all went to his satisfaction. With a great
tramping of boots, accompanied by the tock-tock of high
heels, boys and girls made their way out to the dancing-
floor. The Manager was proud of this dancing-floor.
It was his own idea and with some difficulty he had
persuaded the central management in New York to supply
the necessary dollars. He had been justified in his insist-
ence. The dancing-floor had proved a continuous success.
It had turned his hotel into a night club, which was just
what he wanted. It gave the young officers a place to
dance on, a perfect dancing-floor laid down on the floor
of the desert, on the edge of the canyon. The Manager
thought with pride that no better dancing-floor existed
in the whole continent. He had obtained the flooring
from California; and as for the scenery, that was a thing
that Hollywood itself could not have supplied.

He had got it all flood-lit. If Niagara could be flood-lit,
then why not the canyon? As a natural phenomenon the
canyon scored over Niagara in his opinion. Waterfalls
were always waterfalls, and the fact that Niagara happened
to be bigger than others only meant that Niagara was
more bigly boring. The canyon on the other hand was a
thing on its own. There was nothing like it anywhere else.
The Manager knew that. He did not care much for natural
phenomena, they alarmed him, they were too closely
related to earthquakes and volcanic eruptions and other
natural events with which the civilized world was still
unable to cope. But as a scenic effect they could be
pressed into value.

The central management had boggled for a bit over
the cost of installation (the current of course cost nothing,
ever since Tellussen had discovered how to tap the
electricity in the air). The big reflectors were still expen-
sive to buy and the management in New York had

hesitated. But the Manager in Arizona had convinced them. He had been persuasive, even violent, on the telephone. They had supplied the money and here were the reflectors now, the huge vari-coloured searchlights that swept over the dancing-floor and shot down into the canyon as they revolved and swivelled round.

§

The General Commanding All Troops came ceremoniously to ask Mrs. Temple for a dance. She had been sitting apart, quietly amused, feeling very separate from all these young people having their fun. Her dancing days were over long ago. It tickled her fancy to be asked now for a dance by a General with a bulgy stomach like a ripe gooseberry which would certainly get in the way as they danced. If she dug a knitting needle into it, would it pop? Instead of doing anything of the sort, she rose gracefully and graciously, allowed herself to dissolve into the arms of the General, (she was a slim woman,) and got carried round the dancing-floor four-and-twenty times. There was a certain advantage in dancing with the General: it meant that all the gay young officers and their partners kept out of the way. So she and the General had the floor almost to themselves. He danced badly and his stomach did get in the way, but he danced with great enthusiasm and conducted her back to her chair when it was all over. He delivered her back to her chair with as much gallantry as any Victorian partner restoring an innocent girl to her chaperone.

"I hope you'll be all right, Mrs. Temple?"

"I'm sure I shall be all right, General, thank you so much."

"You understand I have to go and look after my boys? Wouldn't leave you otherwise. Never like to leave a pretty woman alone."

"Dear General, I am sure you needn't worry; I am quite capable of looking after myself."

"Ah, you Englishwomen! Marvellous, marvellous. So competent, so responsible. Well, we all know what you women did during the war. We take off our hats to you; salute you; that's what we do. Must go now. Sure you're all right?"

"Quite sure, General. Thank you for the dance. I enjoyed it."

"Did you now? It's a long time since a pretty woman told me she enjoyed a dance with me. Satisfactory for an old man."

"You're not an old man, General," said Mrs. Temple, seeing him off with thankfulness.

She returned to her chair with a sigh of relief. She liked the General, but it was a relief to be rid of him and to be alone again.

The next person to come and occupy the chair beside her was Mr. Dale. He slumped himself down with a grunt of civility.

"Hope you don't mind my sitting down next to you."

"The General has left the chair warm for you."

"Yes, I saw you dancing with him. I suppose I ought to ask you to dance with me."

"Please don't. There is no need. My dancing days are over."

"So are mine. It is more amusing to watch the young. How decorative they are, like animals. How greatly one prefers the human race when it is content to emulate the grace of animals without bothering to think. Look at those children. Like gazelles, the girls; like young tigers, the boys. The perfect expression of what they ought to be. Fulfilling their functions, severally. The tiger preparing to leap on the gazelle."....

"Now watch. The light is going to turn away from the dancing-floor on to the canyon. Your gazelles and tigers

will be left in darkness for two minutes. How do I know?
Because I know the mind of the manager, clever, horrid
little man. Watch. What did I tell you?"

The light left the dancers and streamed up the canyon
as she had said. A shout of joy went up from the dancers,
vulgar and cheap. The canyon appeared, looking astonished in the sudden illumination more violent than
sunlight or the moon.

"What do you think of all that?"

"It is difficult to say what one thinks," said Mrs.
Temple. "It is of course very beautiful. Theatrical if you
like. But why should one despise the theatrical when
it increases beauty? Such an objection is merely old-
fashioned, surely? Why not make use of modern invention
with an open mind?"

"I didn't expect you to say that, somehow," said Lester
Dale; "I thought you would condemn it out of hand. I
thought you would say they were vulgarizing the canyon."

"It is impossible to vulgarize the canyon."

"Yes, it doesn't lend itself to vulgarization."

They sat in silence and watched. The whizz band
played on. The dancers continued to dance in the darkness. The darkness provided an extra excitement for
them: it was thrilling for them to be on the dancing-floor
not knowing exactly where they were. The lights would
swivel round again at any moment and they would all
be lit up. The kiss would be caught at the moment of
giving and receiving. The music took the place of light,
and suggested the jollity that was going on unseen.

Meanwhile the flood-lighting poured along the canyon,
making the red rocks redder and the purple rocks more
purple; the shadows deeper and more distorted, the
profundities more full of mystery, the shapes more
imaginative.

"If Satan is anything of an architect," said Mr. Dale,
"that is how he has built his Hell."

"On the designs of Gustave Doré?"

"Doré never thought of anything like that," said Mr. Dale, and Mrs. Temple felt rebuked. "No one but God or Satan could ever have invented anything like that."

"You speak as though God and Satan occupied a level position in your mind."

"Well, don't they in yours? Great lords. The lord of good and the lord of evil. What grander position could anyone hope to occupy in the universe? Positively Miltonic. A conception as impressive as the spectacle we are now contemplating."

"You put it in such a way that I don't know whether to take you seriously or not," said Mrs. Temple. "Positively Miltonic sounds to me a very undergraduate phrase. We are both English, you know."

"No, I meant it seriously," said Mr. Dale. Mrs. Temple could not see him, or only as a dim fat lump and that gave more dignity to his voice in the darkness. He went on, "Has it ever occurred to you that by the elimination of one letter and the addition of another letter you can get the attributes of those two supreme persons perfectly expressed?"

"Explain."

"Well, if you take one o away from good you get God; you add one d to evil and you get devil. Q.E.D."

"Is that your own joke?"

"I hope so. I should hate to adopt somebody else's joke and pass it off as my own."

"It sounds to me very much like the sort of joke the hermit once used to make in his novels," said Mrs. Temple, trying to find out discreetly if Mr. Dale knew anything about the hermit or who he was.

"The hermit?" Mr. Dale's voice sounded puzzled.

"No matter. If you don't know about him, you don't. And I won't be the one to tell you. Please go back now to your conception of good and evil, God and the devil.

Do you really believe that two such sharp divisions exist? It is difficult for us to hear each other through all this racket of the Manager's whizz band. Whizz, quite apart from the actual noise it makes, does interrupt consecutive thought and conversation. It staggers ideas; staggers them in the sense that you are switched now on to one idea, now on to another. You cannot ever have anything on a plain level. Whizz makes you feel rhythm, sentiment, romance, youthfulness, cynicism, disgust and excitement all in one. I almost prefer the good old-fashioned jazz. It does not seem to disturb these young creatures in the same way."

"That is because there is nothing in them to be disturbed. They are shells. Shells and semblances. Not an idea among the lot of them, unless you call sex an idea."

"You are rather hard on them, aren't you? What about the young men? They have skill and nerve."

"Oh, you mean with their machines," said Mr. Dale with great contempt. "It has become second-nature to the young. They can no longer help it, any more than the fledgeling can help spreading his wings the first time he is pushed out of the nest. Their skill has become almost a reflex action, in a generation born air-minded. All they can think of is the next war."

"Or of how to prevent it," said Mrs. Temple.

"Don't you believe it. Nothing would please them better than to hear that an enemy force had taken off from Central Mexico. As it may at any moment. Remember Pearl Harbour. Danger is their only justification for existence. So long as they have nothing to fight against they are thwarted, incomplete. Like a woman who has never borne children. They have not fulfilled their function."

"You seem to take a very biological view of human nature. How do you reconcile your philosophy of the purely functional with your ideas of good and evil? If

men and women are what you say they are, surely they
are helpless, fated from birth merely to follow their
instincts, with no design about their lives save the pattern
already traced for them. Yet you seem to regard good and
evil as positive forces."

"I certainly do. Very positive. I never could agree with
the view that evil is merely negation, merely the absence
of good, as darkness is the absence of light."

At this moment the light swept round in a great blade
of gold and flooded the dancing-floor. The dancers waved
and cheered.

"Whether you think them shells or not," said Mrs.
Temple, "you must admit that they are very decorative."

"Handsome young animals. And so prosperous. Everyone in this place seems so sleek, so well-fed. Don't you
get the impression that those people have never known
and scarcely imagined disaster?"

"They are not Europeans, you see. That makes all the
difference."

Both were silent, thinking about Europe.

"They are living on the edge of a chasm, though,"
said Mr. Dale with satisfaction. He looked round towards
the canyon, which was now no more than a black rift
in the blackness.

"Prosperous, as you say," said Mrs. Temple. "Neither
good nor evil, these beautiful young empty-heads of yours.
Just bent upon enjoying themselves and taking what life
sends. Harmless, ornamental, material, shallow."

"They have their discussion-centres, remember. Phi-
Kappa-delta."

"You enjoy exercising your sarcasm on them, Mr. Dale.
I daresay you mocked at their counterparts in England
during the twenties and thirties before the war. I daresay
you thought them equally worthless and shallow, determined only to have a good time. Well, that is perhaps
proper to their age, and you must remember that those

young creatures of ours had grown up under the shadow
of war, their adolesence was darkened even though they
only half realized it, but after 1918 they thought the sun
came out, the sunshine of peace coinciding with their
own youth. I expect you scorned their frivolity then, even
as you scorn the frivolity of these American children now.
Should we not be more tolerant? After all, those merry
ornamental fribbles did change their character in a day
once they got startled into seeing that some things are
serious. They loved life so much that they died for it.
You deride these boys and girls because they have not
yet had a chance of behaving in the same way. Wait
until they do get that chance and then see how they
react."

"You rebuke me severely but deservedly. I expect I
criticize them out of bitterness. You see, I do not like
looking back on the thousands of my own young com-
patriots who gave their lives when they were just coming
into flower. I mind, and my resentment makes me ill-
tempered. It makes me vent my spleen on these poor
young innocent American citizens. It is most unfair.
You are right to rebuke me. My head is bloody but still
I like to analyse these things. So I will say then, that I
exercise my sarcasm on them, as you put it in your
phrase, because they have experienced too little in their
generation whereas we ourselves have experienced too
much in ours. We suffered so much that it remains difficult for us to forgive those who didn't suffer. Wrong of
us, I know; but one is human. You say we should be more
tolerant. It is difficult to be tolerant sometimes; but still
I agree with you that one ought to make an effort. I
think the reason I am so disagreeable about these boys
and girls is that they experienced our tragedies only
by proxy. They didn't live in Europe, did they? They
didn't see their homes bombed; they didn't hear daily
about their villages being shaken down by land-mines.

That makes a difference, you know. It is human nature
not to mind very much about what happens three thousand miles away from where you are yourself. Even we
British never minded, not inside our hearts, not in a
passionate driven-home way, about what was happening
in China during the Sino-Japanese war; we listened to
the wireless rather vaguely, and heard about air-raids on
Chungking, but it never came home to us, not in the
same way as attacks on our own country, our own towns,
our own villages came home to us. China was thousands
of miles away; so how could you expect the Americans
to realize what was going on in Europe, also thousands
of miles away? It all seemed so unreal and so remote.
Even their own disasters didn't take place in their own
country. They had Pearl Harbour, and the fighting in
the Pacific; their ships were sunk, and their men went
overseas; they had scares, when the sirens went in San
Francisco and Los Angeles and Hollywood, and they had
the dim-out in New York and the New England cities,
but what was that? Just a try-out. They never knew what
a blitz meant. They never saw street after street blown
down; they never saw their farmhouses ruined, or craters
appearing in the middle of their corn. Lucky, they were,
not to live in Europe, not to live in Poland, in Rotterdam,
or even in England. They read about it all, yes, they read,
but reading in the newspapers isn't the same thing as
living and dying through it. Oh, they helped, I know;
they helped grandly, they stinted nothing. They came
angrily into the war, attacked and insulted. Then, then
they came in as a roused animal with fangs and claws all
sharp and tearing, angry about Pearl Harbour, angry
about the Philippines, angry about the affront to the
American flag. It wasn't their fault, God knows, any more
than it was ours; it was that invention of the devil which
made us powerless. . . . Of course it can never be used
again; we have the antidote now; its success lay in sur-

prise. But that doesn't alter the fact that America, quite rightly, signed the Pacific Charter or the fact that you and I perch now in Arizona and watch them dance on. To-morrow we may be elsewhere. The one place we can never be is in our own country."

"You take the personal aspect," said Mrs. Temple.

"What other aspect do you expect me to take? Surely we all have talked and thought the thing out until there is nothing more to be said or thought? Such enormous calamities end by tiring the mind. There is nothing left for us but to finish our existence as best we may. We are destroyed; there is nothing creative left for us to attempt. Our chance of constructive days is over. Isn't that enough to make anyone caustic at times?"

Mrs. Temple was not surprised. She had come across other Englishmen who were emptied and bitter, who seemed to have no capacity left for anything but dragging out the rest of their existence.

"It is certainly not pleasant to live in exile," she said.

"Pooh, I don't mind a bit about exile; I always lived in it, so to speak. But then it was voluntary which makes all the difference. Other places always seemed more varied and exciting than England. Even this place, this Arizona with its incredible violence of scenery and this absurd sort of life in contrast, the dancing and the illuminations and what-not, amused me and drew me back for a couple of weeks each year. Then there was China and Africa, oh, and other places I went to. England never saw much of me, even when I was able to go."

"And now that you can't go to England, you want to?"

Instead of answering her question, Mr. Dale leant forward, his hands between his fat knees dangling.

"Look," he said, "the nightly inevitable is happening. The Indians are going to dance."

Mrs. Temple glanced across towards the place where the Indians had their huts, so near to the edge of the dancing-floor that the lights played over them. A little group of them were lounging against their wall, apparently diverted only by the spectacle of the white race dancing, without any thought of dancing themselves.

"Don't worry," she said comfortably to Mr. Dale. "We have both been here long enough to know that it takes some time before they can be set in motion. They have been trained to make as much fuss as a prima donna being persuaded to sing. The greater the reluctance, the bigger the receipts when the hat goes round."

"*Il faut se faire prier*, in fact."

"*Il faut toujours se faire prier pour se faire valoir*, surely?"

Then they both suddenly laughed. It had come as a sort of relief and release to them both to speak a few words in French reminding themselves (even with a pang) of that lost civilization. It brought them closer than any number of words exchanged in English.

"Well, what about these Indians?" said Mrs. Temple who knew when not to insist on the moment. "I suppose they will dance for us in their good time."

"Nothing would stop them," he replied. "That contemptible family which squats permanently over there makes a very good living out of us and out of all the people who buy souvenirs at their wretched shop. Much as I dislike our Manager I must admit that he's good at his job. Do you notice how he has induced the Indians to sell nothing but their own goods? You can buy as many coloured post cards and panoramas and Kodak films as you please in the hotel itself, but there's only native stuff in the Hopi shop, and, at that, he has taught them to make a favour of selling it at all. Why, all new arrivals here are going about in fringed gloves within a couple of hours, slapping their boots with cow-hide whips, and wearing shirts of cheap red satin. Then think of the bedrooms cluttered with rugs and blankets and baskets all in faithful reproduction of the lounge downstairs, and

God knows what other junk gets packed into suitcases for friends in New York."

"It always seems odd to me," said Mrs. Temple, "that there should be such an inexhaustible supply, if the Indians are really as reluctant as the Manager says to part with their treasures. But that doesn't appear to strike any of their customers."

"Oh, the Manager has a very good answer to that question," said Mr. Dale. "Haven't you ever heard him dealing with it? First the Indians put on an obstinate look and become silent; this thrills the client, who describes it afterwards as 'so characteristic.' The mystery of the Indian pleases them as much as what travellers in the opposite direction used to call the mystery of the East. Then finally they suggest that the client should take himself off and get Mr. Royer to confirm what they have said about the unreasonableness of the demand and the impossibility of satisfying it. Mr. Royer is always helpful. He always has time to spare. He asks you into his office. He listens. He smiles with a knowing air which includes both the proud Indian and the urgent customer in his sympathy. He ends by saying that if the matter is left to him he will fix it all."

"And he always does?"

"Yes. But there is a little explanation to be given first. It will be necessary to send a special messenger to a distant encampment of the tribe in order to procure the twin of the rare rug, the special pottery. Naturally, though regrettably, the price will be a trifle higher after a man has had to ride all through the night. . . . Few visitors boggle at this. They are quite prepared to pay a little more for the satisfaction of letting their friends know about that headlong ride, the arrival at the camp fire, the hasty argument, the gallop back with the prize secured. Oh, Royer knows well enough how to provide the story."

"And what happens in reality?"

"In reality, a coffer is dragged out from behind a curtain after the shop has been safely shut up for the night, the selection is made, and by midday the required object is produced. It may be earlier than midday, if the visitor is leaving earlier; very much later if he is making a stay of several days. The greater the delay, and the more prolonged the argument, the greater the value."

"You haven't much opinion of your fellows, have you?" said Mrs. Temple, not disagreeably.

There was a great shout of laughter and chaff. A group of young men and girls had gone over to the Indians, and, taking hold of their hands, were trying to tug them into the centre of the dancing-floor. The resistance was good-humoured and perfunctory; the two Indian women shrieked as they knew they were expected to shriek; the children pattered round in their little moccasins, getting into everybody's way. The patriarchal old Indian stood by, gravely moving his head in feigned disapproval. He had been well coached by the Manager. The flood-lights changed from blue to red, and with the coming of the lurid light a thrum of drums began, beating an insistent time. Feet began to stamp and hands to clap. The American girls threw themselves down, forming a half-circle round the dancing-floor; the college boys and the young officers stood behind them, joining in the rhythm. "With falling oars they beat the time," murmured Mr. Dale in quotation. The Indians themselves were losing their impassivity and were beginning to sway uneasily and to utter hoarse cries,—"They're allowing themselves to get worked up," said Mr. Dale. At that moment the blind man was led up by his attendant and deposited into the vacant chair on the other side of Mrs. Temple. She put out a helpful hand and touched his as it quivered on the crook of his stick. "Mrs. Temple?" he said instantly. "May I sit here for a little? do you mind? Not displacing anyone else, am I?" The attendant retired into the darkness; he was a man with a sour, somewhat Mongolian face, not unlike the Manager. "It makes quite a change, listening to this odd music before one goes to bed," said the blind man. He spoke always with great simplicity, and although his words were sometimes humble his manner suggested only that he was too proud to seek intrusion. He gave the impression of being self-sufficient within his own strange world, touching his fellow-beings only for the brief instant he judged they could endure the embarrassment of his infirmity. Very small were the sips he took at the beaker of life.

"It is becoming a little difficult to hear oneself speak," said Mrs. Temple.

The Indians were indeed fairly launched. Springing into the air, or crouched upon their haunches, or creeping round in circles after one another, their exclamations became more frequent as the drums increased in intensity and rapidity. One could almost believe the savage ritual to be genuine, and the participators to be persuaded of its sacred character. Perhaps like an actor who nightly plays the same part yet always finds a new element in it according to the temper of his audience, this debased and prostituted group of Indians nightly caught some whiff from the outer air, beyond the periphery of lights, and for the moment forgot the semi-imprisonment to which they had sold themselves in the interests of greed.

> "Restore my feet for me.
> Restore my legs for me.
> Restore my body for me.
> Restore my mind for me.
> Restore my voice for me.
> Happily with abundant dark clouds may I walk.
> Happily with abundant showers may I walk.
> Happily with abundant plants may I walk.
> Happily may I walk."

The first dance came to an end and the performers, who had apparently worked themselves into a frenzy, suddenly relapsed into their ordinary state of indifference. They just went back to lean against their *adobe* wall like so many workmen knocking off for the dinner-hour. They had appeared to be extraordinarily moved, and on the instant were moved no longer. The man who worked the lights knew his cue: the red light ran rapidly through the rainbow as the last note was struck and came to rest in a pale yellow which had no more dramatic quality in it than a simple electric bulb. The Indians did not even trouble to pass the back of their hand across their brow to show their exhaustion; by their utter boredom and indifference they suggested that their performance had required no effort either physical or mental. But they had left most of their audience under the spell. Even the youngest and most irreverent murmured amongst themselves.

"Gee! wish I could creep about like that."

"Say, wouldn't we do a spirit-dance in and out among the planes?"

"See, Roy, I know something you don't know." This was a girl speaking. "See those colours they wear? the four boys, I mean? Yellow, green, red, white. Those ribbons round their heads. Well, that's the four quarters of the world. It's a very secret symbol."

"Who told you then, if it's so secret?"

"Never mind who told me; I *was* told, and it's true."

"Well, if it's true, which is which?"

"Just let me think; red is east, yellow is north, green is . . . no, wait a minute, that isn't right; red isn't east though you might think it; green is east. . . ."

"Aw, cut it, Mamie; you don't know and it's no good pretending you do; besides, if it's so secret you shouldn't give it away; why, you might bring bad luck on any of us next time we take off, mixing up all the colours of the

E

compass like that. Ain't you glad we have navigation instruments to check Mamie's directions, Roy?"

"You bet. We'd fly into the canyon instead of over it."

"Who's your wise friend, Mamie? Tell us some more."

"Well, I'll tell you some more since you're so keen. The Earth Magician was floating on darkness . . ."

"Aw, I know that one. Sounds awfully like the Book of Genesis. That the one about making the earth with the help of the white ants? You got that one off Royer. I got it too."

"Bet you she got the one about the quarters of the world off Royer too. He's a gem-quarry, that man."

So they chaffed. Then the drums began again and the Indians crept stealthily out, like cats, to prowl round one another, slowly at first and then with quickening pace.

"You don't usually come to watch this performance, do you?" asked Mrs. Temple.

"No, I don't" said Mr. Dale. "I find these Indians boring. I never did care for Fennimore Cooper, even as a boy. One might perhaps find some interest in the genuine ceremonies; I believe some of the snake dances are very curious."

"Oh, I shouldn't care for that at all," said Mrs. Temple quickly, "even if I were given the chance to go. If these people want to keep their celebrations private one has no right to intrude out of crass curiosity. You may think me priggish, but that is how I feel about it."

"On the contrary," he said, "I don't think you priggish. I think few women would be so scrupulous. Your feeling does you honour." It was a queer little compliment, very unlike his usual manner of speaking. Embarrassed, he got up, and, taking a man by the arm, drew him towards the chair he had just left and made him sit down. The man started politely to protest, but Mr. Dale silenced him with a gesture. Mrs. Temple looked to see who her new neighbour was, and recognized the deaf man. It was no good speaking to him, so she smiled. "Do you mind if I sit here?" he asked, much as the blind man had asked. "Mr. Dale seems to insist on it, I don't know why." He had a lonely, patient face, and he kept his voice so deliberately low that it was sometimes difficult to hear what he said. He had read somewhere that deaf people always spoke too loud.

Mrs. Temple was much amused. She guessed enough of Lester Dale to know that it tickled him to see her sitting between two men, one of whom could not see the violence of the light, and the other not hear the violence of the music. You would need to put them together to make a complete man, and even then would not each one of them lose something of the peculiar world in which they each must live? If she took enough trouble with the blind man she might get on to such terms with him that he would talk to her about his perpetual night. Was it imageless? Did colour exist for him, in some strangely transmuted form? Did sound take the place of colour, so that he might call a harsh sound scarlet and a soft sound brown? She knew that he had been blind from birth. No recollections of a visible world could linger in his mind.

With the deaf man she could never hope to communicate. He wore a pitiable little slate dangling round his neck, and this he would present when he required an answer to a question or perceived that someone was endeavouring to address him, but Mrs. Temple could not feel that this method would take her very far towards intimacy. Not that she desired intimacy with him or with anyone; the warmth had died too thoroughly in her heart long ago, and it was only by a long and painful climb that she had struggled out into her present indifference; but she did wonder what this soundless world could be like and what its compensations were. Perhaps the memory of sounds once heard survived; for, she reflected idly, he can't have been born stone-deaf or he wouldn't be able to speak intelligibly now, only grunts and token-noises. He's lucky in some ways, she thought, as the yowling of the Indians became more discordant.

There was a little stir in the ring of spectators and a bell-hop from the hotel pushed his way through, monotonously chanting "Ge-ne-ral A-dam-son, Ge-ne-ral A-dam-son." "A telephone call," said somebody. The stout General emerged from the ring and was led away, a large vessel taken in tow by a tug. The Indians stopped dancing in their usual abrupt fashion and began going round the circle with a sort of tambourine, jingling a few suggestive coins. People dropped dimes and nickels. The deaf man and Lester Dale both exclaimed "*Please*, Mrs. Temple!" as they saw her about to search in her handbag; and the blind man also exclaimed "*Please*, Mrs. Temple!" as he realized what was going on. "I wonder what Loraine thinks of my three beaux?" she thought, catching sight of the girl who waved back at her.

The General reappeared, accompanied now by a busy young aide-de-camp who ran off and was lost among the pine-trees. The General strolled across with unconvincing nonchalance; he stopped to speak to several people, who agreed afterwards that he did it in order to convince them that he was in no hurry rather than from any desire to exchange remarks with them. Then he saw Mrs. Temple and came to take his leave with his rather ponderous courtesy. "Must be going home now," he said; "late hours don't suit old gentlemen." He puffed a little. Poof-poof. "Hope you enjoyed the show," he added vaguely. Mrs. Temple realized that his mind wasn't on what he was saying and that his pre-occupation was centred on taking his leave as quickly as possible, without drawing public attention to the fact. "My dear General, how right you are, how wise you are. One does need one's sleep. Eight hours at least. Goodnight, General, goodnight."

Tactful woman; charming woman; she doesn't keep on talking when one wants to be off. Thank you. Grateful. She lets me go, doesn't try to detain me; doesn't try to pretend she's got the General at her side. Many women would boast of that. Not Mrs. Temple. She doesn't care. That's why I like talking to her; I know she won't keep me a moment longer than I want to be kept; won't try to get information out of me, information I can't give. Goodnight Mrs. Temple. You're the sort of woman I should like to marry. Men like to marry women, but seldom like them unless they happen to love them. Women bore men, generally speaking, except in bed. You wouldn't bore or bother me, Mrs. Temple, any time, even at breakfast. You would know when to stay quiet. Goodnight, Mrs. Temple, goodnight.

The General's gyro-plane took off with a roar of propellers and soared away across the canyon. They saw it go, with its little red and green lights showing the way it went. It travelled the ten miles across the canyon, from the South Rim to the North Rim. They liked to suppose that the General had gone because he was middle-aged and tired and needed his night's rest; they did not like to suppose that he had gone because he was called away on an urgent message. That was a disquieting idea, the sort of idea that American youth did not welcome; disquieting ideas that did not fit in to the formula they favoured at the moment. Like young England a generation behind them, young America still tried to believe that something might be salvaged out of the wreck of the world.

"It's pathetic, isn't it," said Mr. Dale's soft voice, "to see people making such fools of themselves? That General, for example, such a decent man yet how misguided. Such a poor General commanding troops, yet such a good husband in private life, a fond father probably, devoted, faithful, hard-working, and all the virtues. Why is it that one finds such virtues so dull? There must be something wrong with our conception of social being. In the old days we used to call it human nature, but to-day we demand a greater awareness. It isn't enough to be merely inoffensive. We've learnt that lesson. Vigour, Mrs. Temple. Nothing but the vigour of the mind can fight our battle."

"If anything can fight it."

"We are like people living in darkness in the cellars under a ruined house."

"Forgive me," said the blind man, "I couldn't help overhearing your conversation. I am a Czech; perhaps you know. Technically, I suppose, I was your enemy. In actual fact I suffered as much as you can have suffered. I was in a concentration camp for my insubordinate opinions, and it was not until our conquerors had nothing more to fear that I was released. You remember how contemptuously they let most of us go. I was such small fry, and blind into the bargain, that I was accorded my pass to America without much difficulty. They even provided me with that man whom you have seen leading me about, a fellow-countryman of my own. To make up for the imprisonment I had endured, so they said, he would be subsidized by the Reich. They had taken all my possessions from me; I was quite a rich man once, but now I could not pay an attendant without the assistance of the Reich. It was generous of them, so generous that I have not yet recovered from my surprise."

"Generous indeed," said Mr. Dale, "and very unlike them. May I ask what brought you to Arizona? Was it your own choice?"

"As a matter of fact my attendant suggested it. All places are alike to me, you see, and when he told me how fine the air was and how great his own desire to see the

canyon, I readily agreed. He seems contented here, so I
suppose we shall be making a prolonged stay. Why move?
He describes the beauties of the place to me so vividly
that I can almost behold it. He is an artist in his own way,
a man of notable sensibilities."

"I seem to remember a remark of Churchill's," said
Mr. Dale, "about German tourists admiring the beauties
of the Bulgarian landscape in winter."

"I beg your pardon? I fear I do not quite catch the
allusion."

"Oh, it doesn't matter. It wasn't very important. Just
a thought that crossed my mind. If I may be allowed to
say so, sir, your English is remarkably perfect."

"It is good of you to say so," said the blind man. "I
was Professor of English Literature in the University of
Prague. My accent was my only trouble. Apart from my
accent I think I may say that I know the tongue of
Shakespeare well, but my accent, I fear, would always
betray me for a foreigner."

"It is very slight, and very charming," said Mrs.
Temple. "A sort of lisp. We always think a lisp charming
in English."

"You are too courteous, too indulgent, madame."

"She is always courteous and indulgent," said Mr.
Dale unexpectedly. "If I knew her better I should take
the liberty of telling her that she ought to be more
critical."

"You are telling me now," said Mrs. Temple, amused
again.

"If you knew her better?" said the blind man, surprised. "From the way I have heard you speaking
together I thought you were old friends."

His remark created a short embarrassment, but Mrs.
Temple dealt with it.

"We are old friends only since this afternoon."

There is no flirtatiousness in her answer, thought

Lester Dale, though on paper or on the lips of another woman it might sound flirtatious. But I already know her well enough to know that her intention is merely kindly, a desire to put both the blind man and myself at our ease.

"Being of the same nation in a foreign land makes friendship quickly," said the blind man. He had a gift for little aphorisms. Perhaps that was the result of having been a professor of English literature? Mrs. Temple liked him, Lester Dale liked him too. They were all three quite happy and comfortable together, no strain, no falsity, no pretence. They did not forget the deaf man on the other side; they did not want him to feel left out. Mrs. Temple was careful about this; she turned towards him every now and then, attracted his attention by tapping on his knee, and pointed towards the Indians who had resumed their dance. "Good Lord," said Mr. Dale, "you can't think he wants to watch that hocus-pocus?" "I daresay he doesn't," said Mrs. Temple, "but as I can't talk to him I am doing the best I can." The deaf man seemed grateful; he expressed his gratitude by making some irrelevant remarks. "Yes, it certainly is a very warm evening," he said, "very pleasant to be able to sit out of doors so late. H-r-r-m. H-r-r-m."

"Ask him if he's English," said Mr. Dale.

"Poor man, how can I? he wouldn't hear."

"Write it on his slate."

Mrs. Temple took the slate and wrote, "We think you must be a countryman of ours. English. Are you?"

The deaf man turned the slate the right way up for himself, read the words, and turned towards Mrs. Temple with a pleased look on his face.

"Yes, I'm English," he said in his natural voice, rather loud, then remembering again that deaf men always speak too loud he added very low, "I knew you were both English, you and Mr. Dale. I saw your entries in the

hotel register. I saw you had both put London. I supposed
that we had all come here for the same reason. One has
to go somewhere, hasn't one? A lot of us have come to
America, the lucky ones, those that got away in time."
He seemed as though he would say more, but with the
sudden diffidence of the deaf he desisted and fell back
into silence. His silence was the more remarkable after
his outburst of speech.

Mrs. Temple took the slate and wrote, "I am glad you
are English. I thought you were."

"Oh Lord," said Mr. Dale, "look at those Indians.
Dancing round in the search-me-lights. I suppose they'll
pass the hat round once again. More dimes, more nickels,
more dollars. That tambourine thing passed round for the
second time. I wish I could make as good a living. 'Lo,
the poor Indian!' Low indeed."

"Don't be so scornful," said Mrs. Temple. "You have
admitted that you seldom watch this performance. So
you don't know how it ends. I advise you to wait and see.
It is worth watching, just once. Listen. The drums are
dying down, they are less insistent. The dancers are getting
tired, or pretending to get tired. Soon they will stop.
The moment they stop the lights will change. You know
how well these things are arranged here, like in a well-
ordered theatre. Royer has his electricians waiting for the
signal of command. He has all his people well trained.
Look now: I won't talk to you any more."

As the dance came to an end, and nothing remained
but the last tattoo on the drums, the lights travelled
suddenly round and their beams struck across the canyon.
All eyes followed them. There, poised upon the edge of a
cliff half-way across, lit up as though by the flames of
Hell, stood a wild and solitary figure. His great head-
dress of eagle feathers fluttered in the breeze; his arms
were raised as though in a gesture of invocation. As this
apparition leapt into sight, the drums increased their

volume and the Indians took up an ullulating chant, the stranger because the singers were now buried in darkness. Even those onlookers who were accustomed to the sound and the spectacle could not repress a shudder of excitement as the rhythm quickened; there was something peculiarly suggestive about this combination of the savage music, the primeval scenery, and the ingenuity of modern artifice. The Manager had come out from the hotel and was looking on, because he knew that the theatrical effect was tremendous. He never got tired of this theatrical effect he had arranged. It was his masterpiece. It had cost the central management quite a lot of money, but in the end he had got them to agree that it was worth while.

It was indeed worth while. That savage figure wavering on the cliff's edge, about to plunge, was worth at least ten thousand dollars a year to the central management board. People came from all over the United States to see the canyon and this daimon added something to the canyon's value. What's the good of having a canyon if you don't exploit it?

The Manager exploited it for all it was worth.

The suspense was not too greatly prolonged. It could not be. So breathless an instant could not be sustained for long. With a final yell and a final despairing gesture the coloured figure dived from his height into the depths of the canyon.

"Very effective," said Mr. Dale, yawning and stretching himself. "How is it done? a system of pulleys and wires, I suppose, like fairies in a pantomime, and an invisible net to catch him. Very effective indeed. I quite imagined myself back as a boy at Drury Lane."

With the culmination of the entertainment, a sigh went up from the audience, and after a pause they began to move about; the band played, and there was some renewed dancing. But the party was over, as they thought. At this stage the party was apt to break up and disperse;

there was usually some strolling off into the pine-woods where the budding romances could enjoy a little fairly innocent fun. This evening however things were turning out differently. Word had gone round in a mysterious way, or perhaps it was the General's A.D.C. who had passed it, with a tap on the shoulder and a whisper in the ear. Nobody took it very seriously, or took it only that the manœuvres were to have an earlier start than usual on the following morning. With such big manœuvres going on it was impossible to tell what dispositions would be made next, and of course everybody concerned was supposed to be very discreet. One might ask questions, without any hope of getting an informative answer.

The college girls coaxed their boy friends.

"Now, Dick, you might tell me . . . it won't go any further . . . people say a hundred thousand troops are around here, and ten thousand planes over on the North Rim . . . you might tell me if that's anywhere near the truth."

"I might."

"Yes, but, Dick, you will? Tell just me. No one else. It won't go any further, but anyhow what does it matter? It's nothing but play-acting, our manœuvres. The war's over. They've fixed Europe now. They'll leave *us* in peace."

"There was a time," said the young man called Dick, "when the English used to print U.S.; then they took to printing it *us*."

"I don't get you, Dick."

"No? Well, perhaps you will some day.—Look, pet, I shall be going. See you again before long." He kissed her.

"But, Dick, you haven't answered my question."

"That so? Perhaps I don't know the answer."

He ran off, remembering to blow her another meaningless kiss as he went, but in very much of a hurry to get to the parking place. Inquisitive little bitches they all are, he thought as he went; just anxious to get the low-down on everything, that's all.

He swung his leg over into the cockpit, glad to get away. He felt in a closer communion with his machine than with his girl.

"Contact!" he called out to the groundsmen. "Contact!"

He had never known any such real contact with his girl.

§

Another girl asked questions of her lover, in a different way. They were true lovers, just married; Free French. She had come across to Arizona with him when his orders came to take part in these manœuvres. They were the lovers whom Lester Dale had noted as taking no more notice of this world than if they had been at the North Pole. They lived in a world of their own, as privately as the blind man or the deaf man lived in their own worlds; only their world was a golden cell, not a cell of darkness or of silence. Love, their love, was a room lit by the golden light of closeness and intimacy. It excluded all others. It did not matter whether they were enclosed by four walls or out in the desert. They were always shut in.

"Louis, tell me, why do you have to go? Why do you have to go so suddenly? Is it a sudden order or is it just in the routine? Louis, you *must* tell me. Don't tell me if you aren't allowed to. You know I never ask, but tell me if you can and save me from being frightened. Frightened about your safety.—I am not really frightened; we are both French and we are fortunate enough to be both in America.—America is a safe country, isn't it? The Nazis will never dare to attack America? Louis, look, I am talking now as we used to talk in Europe, years ago. Germany will never dare to attack America, we used to say. Germany will remain satisfied with the conquest of

Europe. So we used to say. Am I talking sense? But Louis, Louis, don't you see that the only thing I care about now is the idea that you, my darling, may be going into danger? And you are being taken away from me! So unexpectedly! I had looked forward to another night with you, to-night. Why do you have to go? Oh why, oh why?"

He tried to soothe her. "*Calme-toi, mon choux, mon petit;* it's just the ordinary manœuvres, nothing else."

"Louis, listen, I love you. Remember that. Remember last night. Nights differ, you know. One loves, always, when one truly loves; but some nights of love transcend even other nights. Last night was a special night. There was the moment when you came into my bed and took me into your arms. I lay in your arms and, afterwards, fell asleep there. Don't forget that. I hoped it would happen again to-night. Now go. If you must go, go. Leave me. Take off in that strong machine of yours, which I believe you love as much as you love France, and fly away across that horrible beautiful canyon. Horrible because it separates me from you, beautiful because it is as beautiful as love or danger and courage. Darling, you will be back here to-morrow evening, won't you?"

"Sure," he said, in English, having picked up the American idiom. He kissed her and ran off, in a hurry to get to the parking place. God, how I love her, he thought as he went.

He swung his leg over into the cockpit, sorry to go.

His plane roared off. They were all going.

§

Other planes took off and departed with the same familiar roar. Soon it could be observed that none of the young airmen remained; the blue uniform was missing from the dancing-floor. At the same time the spread of

whisper and rumour could be observed, that starts from
a spark and runs as rapidly as a prairie fire. No one has
seen the spark fall, but in a matter of minutes the blaze
is a strong violent fact. "Did you see . . . did you hear
. . . someone told me . . . it is said . . . I got it on good
authority . . . the aide told me . . . the General himself
told me . . . the General has been sent for . . . did the
General tell you that? . . . not exactly, he indicated it
though . . . Robert says the General told him he had
been sent for . . . the General got an urgent message
calling him back. . . . What's it all about, anyway? . . .
It must mean something, the planes have gone, the boys
have gone, there's no uniforms left, only college blazers
. . . it must mean something, what does it mean? . . .
there's something brewing down in Mexico. . . . I thought
it was the air fields in Brazil that the Germans had
occupied? . . . yes, Brazil not Mexico . . . in Argentina
too . . . well, I don't know rightly . . . it is all very confusing . . . what about that man who came up from
Mexico this morning with those scarlet flowers? . . . look,
Mrs. Temple is wearing one of them . . . oh, don't you
know? Loraine Driscoll gave it her, Loraine has a crush
on Mrs. Temple . . . well, you never know, perhaps
Loraine is a Quisling and Mrs. Temple too . . . one
never knows . . . in war-time one ought to suspect everybody . . . we never ought to have let the Germans get
those aerodromes down in Brazil. . . . Did the General
tell her that? . . . no, I think it was the Manager told
her that, I'm not sure . . . the Manager says the Germans
have seized the 'dromes down in Mexico . . . what does
it all mean? it must mean something. . . ."

The two English people and the blind Czech and the
deaf man alone took no part in this flutter. Mrs. Temple
looked once at Mr. Dale, and then they both looked at
the blind man who was listening quietly without making
any comment. The deaf man took no notice at all. He

was unaware, inside the silent globe of his private world.

But so far the whispering was only an under-current. The young people continued to dance in a desultory way, though now owing to the dearth of officers some of the girls were reduced to dancing with one another. Mrs. Temple suddenly caught sight of Loraine Driscoll dancing with her own brother. The expression on the girl's face appalled her. Loraine looked like a drugged person; her head was thrown back, her eyes closed, the make-up on her lips was startling across the pallor of her face; she lay helplessly in the arms of her brother. Mrs. Temple, a woman of wide experience, had seldom been more horrified than by this exhibition of mingled terror and sensuality on the face of innocent youth. An unfinished drawing, she had called that face in her private mind: she thought now that she could never feel kindly towards Loraine again, yet the manifest terror of the girl softened her towards the other inexplicable side: should she blame Loraine any more than she would blame the rabbit held by the blood-sucking stoat? She had always disliked Robert Driscoll, Loraine's brother; if she, Helen Temple, had had a daughter she would have travelled a thousand miles to remove her from his neighbourhood. "Dear me," she thought, "the day will come when I shall have to feel sorry for the Driscoll parents if they are really as I described them to Mr. Dale this afternoon."

A bell-hop came out to fetch the Manager. The telephone had been ringing. The staff had answered the insistent bell, offering to take a message, but the voice at the other end demanded to speak to the Manager himself. Royer came in to obey the call, rather crossly, since he didn't like being interrupted when he was on his hotel business. He picked up the receiver as he had picked it up many times only to hear that a party of six or eight was arriving by car at midnight and would require supper, a good supper, an extravagant supper with champagne to wash it down. He was accustomed to these sudden requirements because he always had a lot of reserves in his store and could meet them, but this long-distance call was a different thing. The voice at the other end of the wire said, "We hope you are finding the new bathroom installation satisfactory?"

This was his cue, his signal. He had always foreseen this, but it hurt his heart when the order came. The orders, the code-phrase had come at last. Damn, he thought, it has come. He gave the reply he was expected to give over the telephone: "Perfectly satisfactory," he said, "O.K."

This reply meant that he had understood the code message and would fire the hotel at the pre-arranged hour. He minded having to fire his hotel, but the central management didn't know that. They didn't know that he had any sentimental pride about it; they just regarded him as a manager put in to carry out their wishes, an agent well-paid, a convinced Nazi ready to advance the Cause. They were right in assuming that he would carry out his orders; they were wrong in assuming (if they gave the matter any consideration at all, which was unlikely) that he would carry his orders out in cold blood, in cold unfeeling blood, without a touch of human feeling anywhere within his vile base heart. Yet he did mind. He minded, not only in his own cowardly personal way, knowing that he might be suspected of Fifth Column activities and might get lynched in revenge by those fierce young men to whom he had been serving cocktails at the bar two hours ago, all those cheery and matey clients who might turn nasty at any moment and turn against him, crucifying him with nails driven through his hands and feet; there was no revenge too horrible for them to take if they once recognized him as a traitor; they would cease to be amiable young men; they would

turn into cruel revengeful young men; they would cease
to be the young men who came gaily up to the cocktail
bar saying "Gin and It, please Royer, and make it a
triple." All that happy time was over, finished, done with,
and now nothing was left except his own fear and the
burning of the dear hotel.

He must carry it off gaily. He must not let them think
that anything was going wrong. He must not let them
think that anything very dramatic or important was
happening. He must play up. He was heavily paid to
do so. He came out from the hotel waving a piece of
paper over his head. The lights swivelled across and lit
him up as he came: the neat little Waldorf-Astoria figure
in his black coat. The lights streamed across him; the
hotel electrician was well trained, and the bell-hop had
run out quickly to advise the electrician to light up the
Manager as he emerged from the hotel on to the dancing-
floor. The whole staff had been well trained and their
performance was satisfactory. The sensational effect was
well organized. The Germans had always been good at
organizing dramatic as well as factual effects. And, since
the Manager was in German pay, he produced his effect
theatrically and as though it were entirely in the interest
of the American nation:

"Ladies and gentlemen," he said, "mesdames, mesde-
moiselles, messieurs, I have to announce to you that
military orders have come, decreeing a complete blackout over the whole Grand Canyon area."

§

Blackout. . . . The few Europeans there knew what it
meant. The Americans knew only by hearsay, which is
a very different thing. To the Europeans the announcement came with a greater reality. To them it meant
something they had lived through: the necessity of

F

obscuring windows because if you didn't obscure windows
it meant that a bomb whistled or a land-mine floated down,
destroying homes and cottages or villages or towns or
cities and citizens. It was necessary to put out the lights.
To the blind man it meant nothing because the whole of
his life was blacked-out.

The Europeans knew this. They knew it in their bones
and in their blood. The Americans knew it only at
secondhand. They had heard of the blackout as a banner
headline, but they had never experienced for themselves
what a blackout meant. They had never known the time
when there was no light except in Eire between Siberia
and New York. They had never had to bother about
putting curtains up for themselves in every little home all
over the United States. Least of all had they ever thought
of danger from the air threatening them in the refuge of
Arizona. All had been gay and pleasurable, and now
suddenly this.

Of course everything had been in readiness for years
all over the more vulnerable points of the United States.
The authorities knew all about it, even if the usual
American didn't. The authorities had arranged for a
blackout at a moment's notice, and thus it could quickly
be put into operation at the Grand Canyon hotel, which
was a vulnerable point. It stood right in the centre of the
vast aerodromes on the North and South Rims, and of the
camps where the army in conjunction with the air force
was doing its annual training. If any point in the United
States was likely to be attacked, it was the aerodromes on
the North and South Rims, with the camps arranged on
either side of the Grand Canyon of the Colorado. Why, it
was only a couple of hours' flight from the airfields of
Brazil.

Some of the National Park rangers had appeared by
now, and in their quick competent way were giving
assistance. Mrs. Temple could see one of them moving

rapidly amongst the floodlight reflectors, bending down, removing the big bulbs, disconnecting the flexes. It was clear that each one had his allotted job. The Park Superintendent, his rifle slung across his back, was talking to the Indians. She wondered what the Indians were making of it all; they seemed unperturbed, but perhaps that was because they did not understand. The American girls were all jabbering in little groups, ignoring the efforts of their Miss Carlisle to get them rounded up and shepherded into the hotel. To them the whole thing was a great excitement, a new show arranged for their benefit. They had not yet had time to grow a belief in it; they wouldn't begin to believe in it, thought Mrs. Temple, until they had seen a few people killed.

She thought back over some of the things that had happened during the Second German War. She remembered some bits of the advice she had been given in First Aid handbooks:

"If an elderly man has the side of his face blown away, including an eye, the top part of his nose and part of the lower jaw, and blood, flooding into his throat, is asphyxiating him . . ."

The Second German War had brought these things; it had been bad enough; epic, tragic, none of the big words was big enough to match it; but, huge and murderous as it had been, it was going to appear almost old-fashionable compared with war as it would now be fought.

Everything had gone forward as it were by arithmetical progression. There was an old story of a Sultan desirous of rewarding a subject. The subject asked with apparent modesty if he might be allowed to place one penny on the first square of a chess-board and then to go on doubling it until he reached the last square. The Sultan agreed amid the laughter and derision of his courtiers. How could the foolish man exact so poor a bargain? But when the foolish man had arrived at the end of the chess-board squares, it was found that he had reached a sum the Sultan with all his wealth was unable to pay.

So, speed had gone ahead, doubling itself from square to square. It had gone ahead so fast, that it had outrun prophetic imagination. That men should fly at four hundred miles an hour had surprised the unprepared mind once; but now that they flew at six hundred and some even at a thousand, no one seemed surprised any longer; it was taken for granted and any further advance would be taken for granted too. The capacity for wonder is soon lost. So in the same way did people accept the increased carrying charges of the warplanes. There was no difficulty in accepting that the heaviest bombers could now take off from Dakar, Honolulu, or Rio, arrive within a few hours, unload their bombs on American cities, and get back to their flying bases without refuelling. This meant that any point on the American sea-boards could be attacked by air at any moment, and many points in the interior of the continent as well.

Neither the Government nor the population of the United States relished this idea. They had accepted it in theory, but in practice they had had small experience of either the threat or the performance. They had agreed with the mind, without feeling through the body or the heart. They both resembled and disresembled the inhabitants of Britain in this respect. Britons had lived through certain experiences in the past. They had known the Roman occupation and the Norman conquest, but these events had occurred some considerable time ago, long enough for their effect to have faded out of the popular consciousness. Since then, the moat defensive to their isle had worked well enough. Philip of Spain had threatened it with his Armada; Buonaparte had threatened it again from closer quarters; and in each case, at two centuries difference in time, the invader had been frustrated for different reasons though not without giving a scare to the islanders. An echo of these scares survived in popular phrases: Drake could finish a game, (God bless Drake, we're all right with *him*,) God blew with His wind, (God bless God, we're all right with *Him*;) Elizabeth announced that she thought foul scorn that any prince of Europe should dare to invade the borders of her realm; (God bless the Queen, we're all right with *her*;) and these assurances, oddly justified by events, continued to satisfy the English.

Then after two hundred safe years came Boney. Boney. . . . The English with their traditional gift for turning the terrible into the familiar, diminished the huge small figure of Buonaparte into a nickname of fun. They were frightened of him, so they sought to lessen him. Yet in spite of this lessening, they still kept him as a bogey to menace their children into obedience. The Bogey-man, the Boney man; the Bogey-man will get you; Boney will come and fetch you out of your bed if you aren't good. . . . English children were dutifully alarmed by this threat, and so were English men watching along the shores of Britain for the French fleet from Boulogne to arrive. Boney might come. Boney would come and fetch you all out of your beds as you slept smugly in England on the other side of your moat. The Channel your moat was not so wide as you English might think. To you in your English arrogance it seems impassable. Yet it is only twenty miles wide at its narrowest point; a step, a single stride for the giant Boney in his Continental boots.

Boney was never able to take that step and the English went on in their own way. They had grown well accustomed to the periodic idea of an invasion which never got beyond the other side of their Channel.

Then after more than a hundred years came a change in the menace. It was an important change, but a slight nymph-like figure rose between the surf and the cliffs to meet it, an emanation enriching mythology by a new shape, a twin of Echo, not repeating the exact syllables but speaking new words in the old tone. She did not repeat "We will think foul scorn," but when she said "We will fight upon the beaches" the tone stirred the listener into believing that the words were the same.

It sounded well and the response was gallant. It worked well for a time, but in the end the spirit had been overcome by the gross materialism of armoured force and diabolical invention. Spirit was not enough. Echo was not enough. Echo was out of date. Even the modern twin of Echo was out of date. The twentieth century demanded a more adult nymph to match the century in its forties. The nymph had to grow up and change her character. To be generous and young and Elizabethan no longer sufficed; the brave body had to oppose itself, not to a lance or to a clumsily-directed cannon-ball, but to the extreme and nicely calculated danger of modern science.

Still, death and gallantry remained the same. That could not alter, though the method might alter. Death, thought Mrs. Temple as she hesitated between staying downstairs in the saloon and going upstairs to her own bedroom, death as an event is not really very interesting. It is interesting only as marking the moment of transition between one form of life and another. Indeed it may be argued that life itself, or what we are pleased to call life, is not very interesting either in this world as we know it or in another world where we do not know it but as we suppose it to be. Going further, it is reasonable to suppose that both life and death are of our own invention, framed to fit a continuous state of being which we are incapable of understanding from first to last, from the first painful emergence from the womb to the last painful break. There may be no first and no last, no birth and no death, no life in between, only a continuity which we intersect in a segment like tying two knots in a length of string.

But as these thoughts came into her mind in the confusion of thoughts too large to hold, Mrs. Temple decided that there was no point in remaining downstairs where the chatter made it impossible for her to listen to the silence. She would prefer the solitude of her own bedroom. But she was intercepted several times on the way. Madame de Retz came up to her, frightened. "What is it, do you think, Mrs. Temple? Is it war? Will it be like Warsaw all over again? I was in Warsaw, you know, and then there was Rotterdam, and Belgrade, and London. Will it be like that here? Is it war? Is it? Is it? Can it be so?"

"I'm afraid I don't know," said Mrs. Temple, disengaging her wrist from the woman's clutching fingers. She disliked hysteria. "It may be just a try-out, a test, a practice. I know no more than you do. You heard the evening radio going on in the saloon, and you know it was just as usual. No declaration of war or any hint of it."

"So you think . . . you really think . . ."

"I think nothing," said Mrs. Temple, who had been thinking a great deal, "and if you will take my advice you will go quietly to bed now and sleep while you can without trying to upset anybody else."

"Sleep while I can! You are not serious? You said just now it might be a practice, a test. The American army is on its manœuvres and they must have a practice alarm, no? And you said there had been no word on the radio."

Mrs. Temple was not a cruel woman, but she was badly tempted to remind Madame de Retz that invasion on countries without warning had not been unknown in Hitler's wars. The anxiety in the shrivelled face, however, touched her pity even while it aroused her contempt.

"Of course," she said soothingly, "I expect that by breakfast-time to-morrow we shall all be laughing at the scare they have tried to give us. Goodnight, madame; sleep well."

"Mrs. Temple."

Helen turned patiently.

"Mrs. Temple, if we hear things in the night, may I
. . . would you like me to come to your room? I know
where it is. There are people, you know, who do not like
to be alone. You may be one of them."

I really can't have this, thought Helen; and aloud she
said, "I promise to come and look for you if it seems in
the least necessary."

She escaped at last, leaving Madame de Retz standing
there with her hands clasped over her mouth, staring.
Poor little wretch, thought Helen, so she was in Warsaw,
was she? I see that I shall have to look after her if anything really does happen.

In her bedroom she found Sadie, carefully reaching up
to close the last chink in the heavy curtains.

"How tired you look, Sadie; you ought to have been
in bed hours ago."

"Is it true, Mrs. Temple, do you think? Is it war?"

"What does Mr. Royer say?" She had met Mr. Royer
downstairs and knew very well what he said.

"Oh, Mr. Royer! What does it matter what he says?
What he says will not be the truth. I should not speak so
of my boss, but the time has come when all must speak
out. For me that time has always been, but now I share
it with all."

Helen looked at this girl, who had so often been
touched by the wing of death which brings the truth.

"So you have already made up your mind that it is
war, have you?"

"Surely."

"But, Sadie, you asked me just now if I thought it
meant war, as though you doubted. Now you say 'surely,'
as though you had no doubt at all."

"Ah, Mrs. Temple, dear, you know well enough that
one asks questions when one wants to be contradicted."

"You don't want me to contradict you if I don't believe in my contradiction?"

"Surely not. There are times when truth must be spoken. This is a time. Tell me what you think."

"Well, Sadie, I don't know. I know no more than you do. But I think it is war."

"Yes, so do I. I should leave you now, madame. I have taken up too much of your time already. You have always been good to me. Thank you, madame."

"Sadie, stop a moment. Mr. Royer has taught you to call me madam, hasn't he? Just now you called me Mrs. Temple, dear. I prefer that way of speaking."

"I see what you mean, madame. You mean we are all likely to die now. That is true. We are all the same. Death makes us all the same. I have always known that, because I have always known about death. Death has never been a far-off thing to me, and so one gets used to the idea. The idea comes as a startling thing to people who aren't used to it. People like me who are used to it don't mind. I don't mind being killed. I know I must die soon. I am used to that idea. Death is nothing, once you get used to the idea of losing your life. It is not death one fears; it is life one feels sorry for leaving. It is the only life one has, and one knows nothing else, does one? One knows only what one knows."

"Religious people believe that one has a further life, Sadie."

"Lucky them, then. Yes, I know. I have known good religious people. I have known bad religious people. I have known good people without any religion at all. It has often seemed to me that goodness did not have anything to do with religion or religion with goodness. You are good, madame, though you are without religion. You must not take this as impertinence. It is not the thing that one person should say to another except when life and death come to the meeting-point. Your curtains are rightly drawn now, I think. Goodnight to you, Mrs. Temple, dear, a goodnight."

Helen stood alone in the middle of her room and pressed her finger-tips against her eyeballs. She had sometimes read in novels of people doing this but had never done it herself, except once when a handsome German boy had stuck his bayonet for fun into the entrails of Harlequin her Dalmatian dog. He was a boy who reminded her very much of her own son, the one who had been killed flying; he had the same fresh look and straight eyes; very young. She had said to him quietly, "Why did you do that?" and he had given her a look she had never forgotten. It was meant to be a bold defiant look, but there had been a sudden query in it, as though he wondered why indeed he had committed that wanton piece of cruelty.

Then she had gone away by herself and covered her eyes to shut out the sight as she remembered it and had found the total darkness so simply obtained though not the darkness of memory she desired. A physical blackout, not a mental obliteration, and was now surprised again to find how completely it worked. She had only to apply the lightest pressure and the blackness became total. Everyone, she thought, can try it for themselves. But what they cannot try, she thought, is the whole process which to her was so dreadfully familiar. One has to live through that before it can become part of one's consciousness. "Don't show a light, will you, Mrs. Temple? Government order, you know." Yes, I know. I know better than you know. I've known what it meant. I've lived under these conditions. For years I lived under them. Then I got away, when we saw the war was lost. I was a useless mouth to feed, so I came to America. But I went through the war, Europe's war. I left England only when we were all asked to leave as quickly as possible, not to encumber England when the Peace of Berlin

was signed. Useless mouths; useless women; useless
men. We all came away. Here we are.

Was that danger ever real? she thought. It seemed
extraordinarily unreal now; yet, throwing back her
curtains after first carefully putting out the light—so
strong was the habit in her—it all became real again.
At any moment, she thought, the siren may go off and
the familiar drone of bombers follow it. I got accustomed
to that in England, she thought, but here in Arizona I
must say I didn't expect it. The blackout is ordered . . .
here she gave the curtain a nervous twitch . . . this hotel
has had its blackout prepared for months past, yet none
of us thought it would have to be put into use. We thought
we were safe here in America. "Don't show a light, will
you, Mrs. Temple? Government order, you know." "No,
I won't show a light; I've been well trained in that sort
of thing. Trust me, Mr. Royer; I know well enough what
bombs mean."

"Bombs! I don't know why you talk of bombs. I, Royer,
tell you that I do not know what bombs mean. It is all a
myth in the middle of this jolly life. We are having fun
here at the Grand Canyon Hotel, aren't we? We are
enjoying life. Our young people go down the Bright Angel
Trail and enjoy life there. They enjoy it perhaps more
than you know." He said this with a horrid leer. "Dear
madam, perhaps there are things in life which in your
nice innocence you do not suspect. But to come back to
this order about putting up the blackout, it is a silly
order, isn't it, Mrs. Temple? It is an alarmist order. The
capitals of Europe observed it and some of them got
destroyed in spite of it. I do not believe in this alarm. Let
us all sleep in peace but obey the Government order all
the same."

§

Now she stood at the window looking out, the darkened room behind her. All was extraordinarily still. After the noise of the saxophones, and the laughter, and the chatter, the hush seemed as thick and soft as black velvet. She could not see the canyon, but felt it to be very much there. Some smart head-liner had called it the 100 per cent Maginot line, or America's Last Trench. A trench indeed, some trench! but although no tank could cross it, aeroplanes could fly it. Tanks seemed very out of date now that the battle of America was engaged; tanks which had once seemed to be the armoured answer to all land-fighting in France and Poland, Egypt and Russia. Tanks couldn't cross the canyon, no tank ever constructed could cross that ten-mile-wide-mile-deep mountainous chasm, not unless the Nazis threw a bridge across it, and even the Nazis with all their slave labour couldn't do that quickly enough, not even if they got all the peons of Mexico (which they now controlled) to come up and work for them as the Egyptians were once compelled to build the Pyramids of the Pharaohs.

She wondered in an impersonal way what was most likely to happen. Her mind floated like a little speck above the vision of happenings too appalling for it to grasp. She remembered the same feeling in the last war —already she was calling it the last war!—the feeling that it was useless trying to embrace more than a corner of the huge affair; a sense that the ear-drums would be split and the eye-balls riven by too close an approach to the thunder and the lightning. War might be let loose by human agency, but when it reached such proportions it went beyond control and took its place beside such elemental manifestations as earthquakes and cyclones, where reason and the rational mind ceased to be of value. Only by floating away or else by concentrating on the immediate corner was it possible for the mind to retain its serenity, and with such accustomed familiarity did this system of self-preservation return to her after all these years that she recognized it much as a scent or a touch recalls a familiarity of one's childhood. Precisely these feelings had she known from September the third 1939 onwards. But with a difference. *Then* she had had to learn every step of the way, the progressive stages, the very phrases that would be used, the alternations between the dreadful troughs and the tiny crests, the muted anguish with which one met bad news, the piteous optimism with which one greeted good, trying not to be cast down, trying not to be lifted up, not daring to hope, still less daring to despair. Was all this to be endured again? Could it be endured? or did the soul reach a point of suffering where nothing registered any longer and a numbness like death supervened? True, this time it would not concern her own country, but that did not seem to make much difference : it was humanity just the same and the huge stupidity was the same, the heart-breaking distortion, the abeyance of truths that seemed so plain. For her own part she had no fear; she had no longer anything to lose except her life. Still she could not help speculating on how the attacks would come; from all quarters, she imagined, and as though she beheld a great warning poster she had a vision of the flying fortresses swooping between the skyscrapers of New York, Detroit and Chicago. Perhaps even at this moment. . . . It was strange not to know, but there was no means of knowing: Royer had told her that all radio stations had gone off the air. An expression from the last war came into her mind: Directional beams. She supposed that it would take some little time before the necessary adjustments could be made,—her ideas on the subject were extremely vague,—and before news would again begin to come through.

The confusion in her thoughts was beginning to settle as the first bewilderment passed. She wondered how great the disorganization would be; how well or ill prepared the Americans were for resistance. The vastness of the continent made it seem probable that attacks would be localized and that ' there would be little fighting on land. But she couldn't visualize at all what form this war would take, apart from the air onslaughts that were bound to be delivered on the American cities. Flying the Atlantic was of course nothing to the Germans with modern machines; it was well known that they had constructed aerodromes in the West of Ireland, in Iceland, and in the Azores. The Pacific coast and the Middle West were within easy reach of Mexico. Mrs. Temple smiled grimly as she wondered whether evacuation had already begun and whether the well-to-do citizens were already making for the safe areas. Another last-war expression! It was a shock to find how readily they came back.

There seemed very little doubt that the canyon country would at once become a centre. Obviously the Nazis would lose no time in attacking the air-force so conveniently assembled there, and the troop-concentrations working in conjunction. She supposed that they could scarcely fly the air-force away, leaving the troops exposed without any protection. Besides this, the South-Western command must remain for the defence of the Mexican border. It must be admitted that she had never given much thought to the American dispositions for defence, such things did not interest her, but from stray conversations one inevitably picked up a few scraps of information which might be correct or otherwise. From all that she had heard she was surprised that the raiders had not yet come over.

Would the civilians perhaps be told to leave the hotel? It seemed likely. Closing the curtains again she turned on the light and looked round the room which was the only home she had, the only place on earth where she was even lightly rooted. She never made plans now, what was the good? but she had vaguely intended to stay here until some restlessness should urge her to move. As well be here as anywhere; she had no craving for the life of towns, and the inhuman magnificence of the canyon suited her denuded spirit. She could not have lived in a sentimental landscape; she must have something completely indifferent to human ills.

But now she might have to go. She opened a little jewel-case and took out a small bottle which lay inside. Yes, they were safe, the tablets which anybody else might have mistaken for aspirin. She had often wondered why, in spite of everything, she had not swallowed them instead of troubling to leave England. They would have sent her on a longer journey certainly, but would that have mattered? She had no religious scruples, she was not a coward, and she had nothing to live for. Then why? She could only suppose that the love of life had prevented her and perhaps also the difficulty of deciding when the exact moment had come. "For use in an emergency" the bottle was labelled, but in a series of emergencies one did not seem to be more outstanding than the other. She had kept two things always in mind. In the event of capture she would prefer to die, or in the event of a maiming personal injury.

She put the bottle now into her hand-bag.

She wondered what the hermit would do. He had not been well and she had been worried about him; she couldn't persuade him to come to the hotel and let her look after him; but the message the Indian boy had brought back told her that he was better. She had intended to ride out to him the next day and see for herself, but she supposed that that would now be forbidden. Yet apart from her anxiety about his health she would have

given much for a talk with him. He was, after all, the
only friend she had in the world, if someone so with-
drawn, so separate, could be called a friend. It was rather
like saying No, I haven't got a dog but I do know an old
lion that lives in a cave.

It was almost true to say that the hermit lived in a
cave, though it was not the kind of cave usually asso-
ciated with hermits. It was one of the many cliff-palaces
scattered along that extraordinary region, and for sheer
spaciousness and rude grandeur dwarfed even the palace
of the Popes at Avignon. (Alas, Avignon!) Considered
as an air-raid shelter he would be safe in it; but supposing
a party of Nazis, knowing it to be his dwelling, stormed
into his echoing galleries and drove him finally to bay
against the last wall-face, deep within the earth? She
could imagine him meeting them with his utter cynicism.
She could imagine him giving them a brief lecture in the
last fifteen minutes of his life; Germans, like Americans,
enjoyed lectures, and so would probably squat willingly
on the floor in a semi-circle before him while he with his
back propped against the wall would discourse in his
leisurely scholarly way, moving his fine hands in illus-
tration as he had moved them in the lecture halls of
Oxford and Cambridge, Bonn and Heidelberg, Harvard
and Yale. He had always known how to fascinate the
young. The fascination had never depended on the
elegance of his person but on the elegance and the semi-
humorous gravity of his mind; indeed, his personal
appearance, which had always been singular and had now
become even more remarkable since his long retreat into
the Painted Desert with no devoted woman to tidy him
up, would add to the towering spectacle of this once
famous philosopher, stylist and novelist addressing his
last audience.

"Gentlemen," he would say, or "Meine Herren," for
he knew German as well as he knew English and would

address them in their own language, "I ask you for a quarter of an hour only. A quarter of an hour may be spared even from a Blitzkreig or War in a Hurry. I should be sorry to see the representatives of modern Germany take their departure from this interesting and ancient abode of man (now mine) without the benefit of a few comments from me. Those comments may possibly lead some of you or your brothers or cousins to return to a study of these cliff-dwellings inhabited perhaps by a pre-Indian race and certainly by a race of men living here before the North American Continent had the misfortune to be discovered by the Europeans,—or should I say before the Europeans had the misfortune to discover the North American Continent—not by Christopher Columbus, I may remark, since Columbus, contrary to popular belief, never landed in North America at all. I regret this apparent denigration of Columbus since as a sailor of Genoa you must regard him as an Axis partner, but my respect for the truth must not be allowed to desert me in this my last quarter of an hour of life.

"I fear that I am digressing, gentlemen; you should recall me to my task more abruptly instead of encouraging me by your courteous laughter.

"I was saying, was I not, that these cliff dwellings were of the highest interest both to the antiquarian and the geologist; I need only invite your attention to some of the flint chips you will find lying within your reach upon the floor, to secure your agreement with J. W. Powell that these caves were once the home of some old arrow maker. Concerned as you are with weapons of a different type, primitive toxophily doubtless makes but a limited appeal to you, nor would I desire to waste the time of busy men with a philosophical discourse on comparisons which could lead only to the most trite reflections. I cannot refrain however from pointing out the traces of primitive art which you will already have observed upon

my walls. You have a torch? Yes. If you would kindly
flash it across the wall. Just over here; thank you. The
design is very spirited, is it not? To my mind it recalls
certain miniatures of the Mughal school of the early
seventeenth century, but I must not waste your time or
mine over such comparisons; I would only ask you to
notice the mountain lion or cougar crouching to leap on
the spotted fawn of the Kaibab mule deer, *Odocileus
hemionus macrotis*, while a squirrel chatters in the branches
of a tree overhead. You will not fail to recognize the tree
as the Ironwood, *Ostrya Knowltoni*, which as you are
doubtless aware was presumed to be extinct until 1889
when F. H. Knowlton discovered a specimen near the
end of the Hance Trail. The squirrel, as you will also
have remarked, bears a strong resemblance to our local
white-tailed species *Sciurus Kaibabensis*. It is possible that
in your somewhat precipitate journeyings over, not
through, the Grand Canyon of the Colorado you have
had little opportunity for observing the characteristics
and pleasing antics of this unique little creature. You
will appreciate that I use the word unique advisedly. I
have always in my life been careful to use words according to their proper meaning. Therefore when I say unique
I mean unique, and now especially in relation to this
squirrel. The fact is that owing to the cutting of the
Canyon on one side and to the deserts on the other
three sides the white-tailed squirrel of the North Rim
and its relation the Abert squirrel of the South Rim
find themselves isolated from the rest of the world.
They exist nowhere else.

"But, gentlemen, you must not allow me to run away
with these accounts of facts which for many years have
entertained the leisure of a recluse. You must allow me
only to remind you that the botanist also may pursue his
studies here to his advantage; in fact, should any of you
number a botanist among his acquaintance I would

beseech you to remind him of the seeds of the giant lima bean which, discovered among the pots and shards in a dwelling on Bright Angel Creek, were persuaded to germinate and come to life after centuries of an apparent death. I mention this because I have a notion that other forms of plant life, now lost, may yet be restored to cultivation by a determined searcher. Your nation, gentlemen, if you will permit me to say so, includes traits of character which do not find favour among the European or the American peoples. Yet as an observer leading my chosen way of existence, an existence so soon about to terminate at your hands, I must also pay tribute to the extreme thoroughness which you are accustomed to bring to your scientific as well as to your military undertakings. It is for this reason that I should wish you not to neglect the possibilities of dormant-seed investigation in the Colorado region when the conclusion of the present war allows you to turn towards such interesting matters.

"It will scarcely be necessary for me to remind you either of the existence of those caves or of the extravagant proportions they sometimes attain. You, meine Herren, who are accustomed to creating the works of man on so imposing a scale are perhaps less apt to be impressed by the works of Nature. You may feel that by your engineering ingenuity you might produce caves such as the one you are now sitting in. Dynamite would do it. Yet let me remind you that the processes of Nature, slower than yours it is true, work more exquisitely. Let me, for example, remind you of the cliff-dwelling on the Mesa Verde, which is sheltered by a cave over four hundred feet long. Here, also, you will find mural paintings which I would recommend to the attention of your photographers.

"Meine Herren, war bores me. Like all rational men I have always preferred ideas to bombs. Although I have

never regarded myself as a man of science and have never
been regarded as one by any of my more serious contem-
poraries,—ah, I notice your derisive applause,—I can
assure you that in my amateurish way the advance of
scientific discovery always interested me but that I
invariably found myself in sympathy with the constructive
rather than with the destructive type. It seemed to me
far more useful far more interesting, to expend several
millions of money on medical research than on the exploit-
ation of engines of war. You may possibly regard me as old-
fashioned, you young men to whom war is an excitement
and an adventure. I should not blame you; indeed, I have
not the time at my disposal to expound my reasons for
blaming you or for explaining my reasons for finding you
completely at fault. You, as one of our English poets
remarked some time ago, have the gun and I have not.
Besides, I am for the moment your host; and one of the
first duties of a host is not to delay his guests beyond the
term when they would wish to remain. Even at this hour
I should not wish to be found lacking in courtesy.

"I will not detain you much longer. I was remarking,
I think, that I had always preferred ideas to bombs.
That was one of the reasons which induced me to leave
my own country, England, for America when the last
war started. My country-men blamed me. They called
me a rat leaving the ship that didn't intend to sink. No
worse name could be given, even to a rat. I accepted that
reproach. I preferred to carry civilization into its last
retreat, which I took to be the United States of America.
In my vanity I believed that my mind was of more value
to the world than my mangled body under a heap of
debris. It was not physical cowardice, believe me, which
induced me and some of my friends to abandon our
threatened island for the greater safety of Arizona; it was
the conviction that if civilization was to be carried on at
all, we were the people to do it. A mistaken idea perhaps,

and your arrival here now demonstrates the fallacy. There is no escaping you; like locusts you invade every corner of the earth. Ah, you growl at that; you become threatening. Bear with me one moment longer. That which I have to say in conclusion cannot fail to afford you a certain satisfaction, since it is the last pronouncement of a man who despite his nationality and his pacific temperament did genuinely and without prejudice endeavour to consider your point of view and to appreciate it on such merits as it might be found to possess. And what did he find? He found a fanaticism which might almost qualify as religious, since it is possible to argue that the blindness of belief in a creed may be applied equally to the principle of good and to the principle of evil. You may argue moreover that the passionate desire for the glory and aggrandisement of your nation cannot be considered as a principle of evil and that it all depends upon the point of view. This argument may have been tenable once; but it is no longer tenable in days which should be, even if they are not, more enlightened. The pity about your fanaticism, meine Herren, is that its vigour and efficiency engendered not only the healthy constructive principles but also the dark passions of rapacity, brutality and mendacity in your own country and the dark unwelcome passions of hatred and revenge in others. This was the pity and the evil you brought upon the world. You used, not black magic, but black competence, and let me pay you the tribute of saying that you did your job well.

"I admire you, representatives of young Germany. I admire your Führer who has taught you how to act.— No, you need not cheer at the mention of his name. You need not make these caves resound with your Heil. The tribute I render to your Führer is the tribute I might render to the mediaeval Devil if I believed in him: a prince of darkness who mighthave been a prince of light.

"My young friends, no, I suppose I mean my young enemies, one last word. I promise you that this shall really be the last. Recently an English lady of my acquaintance who occasionally has the kindness to visit me in this somewhat remote retreat, brought with her a copy of one of my own works. As a rule I dislike being reminded of anything I have written, since I find that less than a year later I have revised my ideas to the extent of not believing in them any longer, if, indeed, I ever believed in them at all. On this occasion, however, I could feel no resentment since I can trust the lady to whom I have referred not to remind me of anything I should prefer to forget. I will read the passage to you. I had written it in 1937, some years before you ever started the second German war, the Naziwar, and before I had ever found my personal refuge in these cave dwellings which you have now in your ever-increasing tide invaded.

"The passage, I think, is apposite. I suggest that you might consider it as a signpost for your future conduct. Ideologically the passage still seems to me to be sound. This is what I wrote:

" 'The inhabitants of the high-lands of Arizona are cut off from one another by the mile-deep abyss of the Grand Canyon. But if they follow the Colorado River down towards its mouth they find themselves at last in the plains at a point where the stream can be conveniently bridged. Something analogous is true in the psychological world. Human beings may be separated by differences of intellectual ability as wide and deep as the Grand Canyon, may peer at one another, uncomprehending, across great gulfs of temperamental dissimilarity. But it is always in their power to move away from the territories in which these divisions exist; it is always possible for them, if they so desire, to find in the common world of action, the site for a broad and substantial bridge connecting even the most completely incommensurable of psychological universes.'

"Those phrases written in 1937 hold good to-day. Wide as is the gash between our mentality and yours, between the captive peoples and the Nazi swollen with conquest and vainglory, I must persist in my belief that the day will come when we travel on our opposite rims down the canyon of misunderstanding to meet at last on those plains where the river can be conveniently bridged."

Some applause broke out, as at the end of a lecture. These fierce youths had been students once, and as students had been regimented into expressing approval of a lecturer they had enjoyed. Habit and training were strong in them, even in such peculiar circumstances. But the hermit gravely bowed, and in his bow he managed to convey all the scornful courtesy of a vanished Europe:
"Den Dank, meine Herren, begehr ich nicht."

§

Mrs. Temple had got herself completely carried away on this imaginary picture of the hermit faced by a gang of young Nazis. She was already beginning to feel sorry about his being shot, when the siren went off.

It was just like an English siren. Just the same wailing cry. She had somehow expected it to have an American accent but it was the same note as she had heard rising and falling across London, across Sussex, across Cumberland, across Wales. Why, oh, why, she thought with an sudden anguish of anger and pain, why couldn't these ingenious Americans have devised a siren of their own? Not reproduced exactly the same sound that we endured during all those years? They had copied us,—they who had known nothing of our suffering or our temper or our fear, nothing of our destroyed cities and villages, nothing of our cratered pastures, nothing of our crops and forests set alight, nothing of our men and women who went out night after night fire-beating to save our harvest, nothing of our men and women driving madly through walls of fire in our cities to save streets of flame when the water-supply had given out. What did the Americans know of this? They knew nothing; they had never experienced it. They had helped us, yes, with material, with bombers, with their Lease-and-Lend Act; they had been fine allies; yes, splendid, helpful; but, in the last resort, they had never had the real thing in their own country, not the real thing poked home at them; not this real thing that was now coming at them and which they now encountered by an imitation of the English siren-blast—Whoo-oo-oo Whoo-oo-oo Whoo-oo-oo, dying away gradually like the cry of an owl, a fading-out, and then a waiting for death to descend.

§

There they were. Vroom, Vroom,—the desynchronized sound of bombers. Distant, high-up. It would continue for what would seem an interminable time, and she remembered how before the beginning of the last war one had tried to comfort apprehensive people by saying that an aeroplane flew very fast and would be gone almost before one knew that it was arriving. The Americans at least would not make that mistake; they would know that one caught the sound from miles away; they would know also that when one wave had passed another wave would follow it and that the sky would be a gigantic hive throughout the night.

What ought she to do? It was so wearisome to have to start the whole thing all over again! She must be active, now that it had really come. They were in the very centre of the obvious objectives; there might be casualties in the hotel itself; she must do what she could. She thought back on the life she had led during the last war. First aid. . . . Had any provision been made for that? She must go down and see what was going on.

She found the lounge downstairs full of people. Some of them were still in their evening clothes, others in dressing-gowns. She noticed that they were all standing up and moving about, a sure sign of nervousness. There was a crowd round the cocktail bar, and such was the pressure of business that Royer himself was helping to serve drinks. But his hands were shaking and he had to keep mopping up the counter.

Mrs. Temple slipped out of the front door, which had been shrouded now by a heavy curtain.

It was pitch-dark outside, or so it seemed to her until her eyes became adjusted and she saw that the enormous Arizona stars were giving a little light. She walked to the edge of the canyon and stood there until its sculptures began to detach themselves and the great darkness of its profundity was scooped into the night. The vrooming of the bombers was unmistakable. There were two Presences in the night: the certainty overhead and the mystery at her feet. She listened to them both; absorbed them both; and then crept into the hotel again, pushing the curtain aside as she had often pushed a curtain aside, entering a Roman Catholic cathedral somewhere in Europe.

The lights of the hotel lounge met her. The talk of the people grouped there met her. They were all trying to be gay and brave. She could see that they were all puzzled and frightened, pretending not to be. Vroom, vroom, vroom, went the bombers. Madame de Retz saw her and came up to her.

"You hear them?"

"Well, madame, of course I hear them. We all hear them. We have heard them hundreds of times, you and

I. We are accustomed to these sounds. You and I, who are experienced, must make ourselves useful to those who are not accustomed. I shall rely on you to help me."

"Mrs. Temple, I cannot. I cannot help you. I am a broken woman. I have seen too much horror in Warsaw and other places. I am broken, I tell you, I cannot help. You English, you are tough, you have no imagination. You stand things, you do not become haunted as we Slavs become haunted. We Slavs, we will fight to the death; but if we do not have the good fortune to die, we live on in a mystical life it is impossible for you English to understand. . . ."

"Nonsense," said Mrs. Temple; "I understand your mystical life quite as well as you do. But I do know that there are times when the mystical life has to give way to the practical life. I regret it, but there it is. So, now, do allow me to rely on you for help if I need it. I know you won't fail me."

She knew that Madame de Retz would fail her, at once, and in the slightest emergency; but this brisk way of treating Madame de Retz seemed to be the only way of saving her from immediate hysteria.

"You have brought your parrot down with you, I see."

The bird was perched on her shoulder, attached to a bracelet on her wrist by a long slim silver chain.

"Grigori? Yes, I could not leave him. He is my pet, my little boy. I could not leave him to be frightened alone in my bedroom. Have you children, Mrs. Temple?"

"No," said Helen, having lost her only son.

"Ah, then you would not understand. The anxiety one feels. The need to give all the comfort possible. I know a bird is not quite the same as a child, but he is all I have. You have not even that, my poor Mrs. Temple."

Grigori screamed.

"No," said Helen, "I haven't even that, thank goodness."

Grigori screamed again.

"Bright Angel Trail," he shrieked this time, so distinctly that many heads turned towards him.

"Listen, listen!" cried Madame de Retz, once more clutching Mrs. Temple by the wrist in the gesture that Mrs. Temple so particularly disliked. "He is a prophet, listen. He warns us. He says 'Bright Angel Trail' always when there is danger. He knows. Grigori knows. I know. I told you we Slavs had a mystical life. You said you understood it but you don't. English people don't. You have no mysticism, no religion. You have common sense only. Useful, yes. But dull, dull, dull. The only time when you have religion is when you are Roman Catholic, and then you are Irish: and when you have mysticism you are Scotch."

"Dear me," said Mrs. Temple, "that's rather sweeping, isn't it? and Grigori isn't a Slav, anyhow."

She wanted to get away from the Polish woman and the beautiful disagreeable bird on her shoulder. She had a great respect for the Poles, but Madame de Retz did not seem to represent them as she should. She was a bad specimen; a poor representative.

Mr. Dale came up, attracted by the noise the bird was making. Mrs. Temple wondered if he had come to her rescue.

"Well, madame, is the proverb true of your parrot: 'He says nothing, but thinks the more'?"

Madame de Retz replied seriously, "I do not know what he thinks. He says much. He says 'Bright Angel Trail.'"

"Is that saying much, madame?"

"It is saying much for those who wish to hear."

§

"Lord," said Mr. Dale moving Mrs. Temple away into a corner of the lounge, "what a bore that woman is. So intense. And her horrid bird."

"Yes, but now look here," said Helen hurriedly, "don't bother any more about Madame de Retz, let us think instead about what we ought to do. I don't want to be officious, but there are planes overhead and we may get bombs at any moment. We must ask Royer what arrangements he has made."

"I don't trust Royer."

"Nor I, but there is no one else, unless we could find the Park Superintendent."

"I have already looked for him. He has gone out to the aerodrome. After all, that is what matters; we are only a handful of civilians here; we don't count."

"Only to ourselves."

An explosion came; it was very muffled, but everything in the lounge rattled. Women grabbed at each other, and waited expectantly for the next bump.

"That was a long way off," said Mrs. Temple.

"On the other side of the canyon, I should say,—ten or twelve miles at least."

"What will happen if they drop bombs into the canyon itself?"

"It will wake some fine echoes," said Mr. Dale, "and some fine pieces of rock will go flying about. With any luck we may be there to see it. If things get too lively up here, or if the hotel gets destroyed, we may all have to take refuge in that dug-out provided by Nature. I think I should pack a little suitcase if I were you, Mrs. Temple. Meanwhile shall we go outside and see what is going on?"

The planes were louder and searchlights were fingering the sky. Suddenly a large yellow square of light appeared in the blackness of the hotel, and another, and another, and another.

"Good God," said Mr. Dale, "it's the landing-window and the windows of the corridor, look, the whole row of them. They must have forgotten to draw the curtains and someone has switched on the lights."

"The curtains *were* drawn," said Mrs. Temple, "and the lights were on as I came downstairs. This is deliberate. It's a signal. Come!"

She pushed the curtain back and let it fall behind them.

There was an uproar in the lounge, a crowd of people gathered round one gesticulating figure in the centre. Royer it was, shouting at the top of his voice while the crowd of his guests surged round him. The man was in a frenzy and the only people who appeared to be trying to protect him were the three white-coated negroes from the dance whizz-band. Blows had been struck already and there was blood on their coats. Two of the Park rangers were there, struggling to get at Royer.

"Aha!" the Manager was screaming, "I hold you, enemies of my Führer. I die with you but you die too. I show our boys the way. My lights show the way. Then comes the bigger light, the beacon, the column of light, the fifth column. It roars up, red, tall."

"What on earth does he mean?" whispered Mrs. Temple. They were standing near the door, away from the hurly-burly.

"The man's possessed," said Dale, "and he's going to get lynched if his niggers can't save him. The little worm, I wonder where he ever found the courage. I think you had better go to your room, Mrs. Temple; you can do nothing here and it is not going to be a pleasant sight. If you like, you can help me to darken that landing and the corridor. That ought to be done and done quickly if no one else has thought of it. Come."

They skirted the stormy crowd and reached the stairs. Fat little Dale went up so quickly that Helen in her long frock could only just keep up with him. She tripped over her frock, following him. She was grateful to him

for taking no further notice of her at all. He had coaxed
her away from the lounge and now she must look out
for herself. She was grateful to him for respecting her
independence now that he had done all that a man
should do; getting her away from the unpleasant sight
of Royer being lynched.

On the stairs Dale collided with the attendant of the
blind man. He came tearing down the stairs at so wild
a pace that he might have been blind himself.

"Here, steady," said Mr. Dale, holding him up, "where
are you off to? What about those lights along the landings?
Why haven't you put them out? Why aren't you looking
after your employer? Surely he needs you? He's blind,
isn't he? Hadn't you better go and look after him? Well,
go then," and to Helen's astonishment Mr. Dale gave
him a push which sent the man rolling in somersaults
down the stairs, ending up with a groan at the bottom.

"Mr. Dale, you may have broken his leg."

"What is a leg, when violence is loose? There is a man
down there being killed, Mrs. Temple: Royer our Manager is being killed now. He is being pulled to pieces by
our civilized crowd. The young men have got hold of
him. The young women have got hold of him too. They
are not separate young men or women; they are a mob:
mass-hatred has seized them. They are wilder than those
Indians we saw dancing after supper to-night. They are
as ruthless as those young German men flying the 'planes
we hear overhead. Come, Mrs. Temple; don't stop to
think about the traitor whose leg I may have broken;
that traitor, that creature of Royer's, that Quisling, that
wriggling worm in the fine land of Arizona; don't think
of him; don't listen to those appalling cries rising up
from below; only come with me, and shut out the lights
which may give guidance to the enemy."

He was already on the landing, twitching the curtains
into place, when Sadie came.

"Mr. Dale, Mrs. Temple, we're on fire."

"On fire?"

"The hotel's on fire. Royer's friend, the blind man's attendant, started it. I saw him doing it. Get out quickly, both of you; it's all wood; it'll go quickly. I think he's Royer's brother. He looks so like him. Come; run."

They ran downstairs, the three of them together. At the bottom of the stairs the blind man's attendant lay tumbled in a heap, moaning. In the centre of the lounge Royer lay dying, while his murderers stood round, appalled now that they had accomplished that which they had wished to accomplish. The three negroes of the band were there, still alive, still standing over the body of their fallen boss; their white coats were patched with blood, they were swaying on their feet, but they were calling out in a sort of incantation:

> "He said we'd get our rights,
> He said we'd get our rights,
> He said we were good Americans,
> Good as any other Americans;
> He said we'd all be good Americans
> If only Hitler came in."

"The negro fifth-column too," said Mr. Dale, pausing to look at this drunken body-guard; "no wonder Royer could make an appeal to them. Poor devils. Look at their rolling eyes. They look so mad now, that you might think the whole future of America lay in their keeping. God knows whose hands it does lie in, but certainly not in theirs. Come along, Mrs. Temple. You can't do anything for Royer; he's dead by now. And there goes another bomb, nearer this time. Come away from this place."

"Where to?"

"Into the canyon. Where else? But we must take the others."

Helen saw him scramble up on to the cocktail bar, an

astonishing sight. It reminded her of the orange-box preachers near the Marble Arch, The fat little man dominated the lounge from that ridiculous elevation, and as he raised his hand demanding silence, silence fell. They were all so distraught and leaderless that they would have listened to anybody choosing to take command.

Even so, she marvelled at the way he got them all to obey him. He had to tell them that the place was on fire and that he could allow none of them to go upstairs to rescue any of their possessions. "Take the rugs and the cushions from here," he said, making a gesture round the lounge; "take what you can for your comfort. Look here," he said, turning round to the back-dresser of the bar and handing out bottles to the men, "stuff these into your pockets,—help yourselves,—take the brandy and the whisky for choice,—leave the liqueurs." The men made a rush and stripped the bar in an instant. "Take cigarettes too," said Mr. Dale, flinging the packets in handfuls on to the floor. "And matches," he added, hurling matches after them. "No torches," he said angrily, but then discovered a whole drawerful and distributed them to the hands stretched out to receive them. "Save those batteries," he said, "you'll need them later. Economize them.—Mrs. Temple!" he said sharply, "take all the women into the larder, scullery or whatever you call it, and collect all the foodstuffs there, tinned, canned, and what not. Get the women away and meet me outside this place within fifteen minutes with everything packed into baskets ready to carry. There are heaps of native baskets stacked in the Indian huts. Get the Indians to bring their baskets out; get the Indians to help. Frighten them into obedience, only get them to work for us. Frighten them with something more immediate than a bomb or the fire breaking out on the hotel."

Mrs. Temple listened to all this; she was standing near

the cocktail bar with Royer lying dead and messy at her
feet. She was ready to obey Mr. Dale, but responsibility
for the blind man worried her. She took the blind man
by the hand and said very gently "Will you come with
me?" He recognized her by her touch and came willingly,
trusting himself to her. She said, "I cannot lead you
down into the canyon myself, because I have something
else to do, but I am going to put you into the charge of
another person whom you can trust as you would
trust me."

He showed no surprise at the suggestion that she should
lead him down into the canyon, nor did he ask where his
attendant was. War, to him, was a thing which brought
such strange disjunctions about. He was used to it. He
accepted it.

"That's all right, Mrs. Temple; if you say I can trust
somebody I'll trust them."

Mrs. Temple beckoned to Sadie.

"Sadie, I want you to take charge of this man."

"Mrs. Temple, sure I will."

"Take him outside the door, then, and wait with him
there till I come."

"On to the dancing-floor?"

"That is right; on to the dancing-floor. Let him sit
down on a bench and sit down with him yourself. Don't
leave him. And if bombs should fall . . ."

"English lady," said the blind man, interrupting, "if
bombs should fall, I know what to do. Remember, I have
been in Prague. Throw yourself flat, put your handkerchief
between your teeth, raise your chest from the ground,
so that your lungs don't burst and your teeth don't
break . . . it sounds horribly familiar, doesn't it? We
both know about it. *Quo res cunque cadent, unum et
commune periclum, una salus ambobus erit.* However things
may happen, there shall be to us both one common
danger and one source of safety. I will take charge of

H

my guide as she will take charge of me. We will trust each other, as we both trust you. Come, my guide, let us go as the lady tells us to go."

Mrs. Temple waited just long enough to see the professor and the waitress making their way out hand in hand towards the dancing-floor where they would throw themselves flat if bombs should fall.

The hotel caught properly alight shortly after this and blazed as only well-dried pine-log timber can blaze. Poor, dead, cowardly Royer, being rapidly cremated with the floor of the lounge he had been so proud of, could not have been better pleased at the success of his laid scheme. "I can't help feeling sorry that Royer isn't here to watch his bonfire," said Mr. Dale to Mrs. Temple as he helped to guide their fellow-guests by the glow-worm light of torches towards the head of Bright Angel Trail. "He would really have enjoyed it so much. Though, of course, he would have hated it in a way. All his precious hotel destroyed. He was an artist in his own way, that man. Let us respect him, Mrs. Temple. *De mortuis.*"

The hotel then shot flame into the air. It was very fine and grand in its death, far finer and grander then it had ever been in its life. The procession of hotel guests making their way towards the refuge of the canyon turned their heads over their shoulders to look at this funeral pyre which represented not only the last thing they might ever see of what they called civilization but also the last of their own personal possessions. Each of them began to think of things left behind. . . . None of them had any luggage at all, not even a parcel; they were all stripped bare.

§

The flaring light from the hotel fire made the torch light unnecessary, and Mr. Dale shouted back over his shoulder that all torches should be switched off. "Save those batteries," he said as he had said before; "you'll need them later." They obeyed him and marched on behind him like a regiment following its commanding officer.

The red light of the blazing hotel lit the night into a hellish resemblance to daylight. It lit up the night into a redness as bright as the yellow sunlight of day. Extraordinary shadow-depths appeared in the canyon, and the colours of the canyon rocks were called into being also, as though they had been asleep and were now in the middle of the night suddenly startled back into the colours they always held. Yet these colours and shadows were intensified by the fire to a degree they never knew beneath the diffused light of the sun. The architectural shapes became more like architecture designed by man, intentional; the colours more like a painter's colours, but with a strange and particular violence of violet and vermilion, cobalt and saffron. The blazing hotel was dramatic enough in its own way but the magnificence of the canyon cheapened it into a mere little bonfire. The quick disaster of man showed up cheaply against the slow carving of Nature.

It was an odd train of people that began to descend slowly into those depths, though no odder probably than any assortment thrown together haphazard.

§

A big crash occurred just as they reached the head of the trail. It seemed as though all the rocks of the canyon must have been thrown sky-high, to fall shattered into place again with a reverberation that echoed from Arizona into Utah. The echoes went on, bounding from temple to temple, from cliff to cliff. The air shuddered; the sound rolled up and down those hundreds of miles cleft in the earth. Madame de Retz gave a little cry of distress: Grigori, whom she was carrying perched on her shoulder, toppled off. He was dead. He fell in a small soft heap at her feet, killed by blast. She picked him up; she expected to find him warm and feathered still. Then she discovered that his little body was completely naked, stripped by blast of the feathers that had made him so beautiful. No longer green and red and plum-coloured, but just a pink naked body, pathetically plain and light in the hands. She turned him over and over in her hands, trying to find something of the beauty that had once been Grigori. Nothing was left of that beauty. Nothing but a stripped ugliness was left.

She carried his poor little naked corpse carefully down into Bright Angel Trail. A bird's body is very light. What Madame de Retz did not realize and what the others did not realize, was that they had all been killed on their way to the head of the trail. Grigori had died outright because he had no soul.

The others went on. They had to go on. They had to complete their fate in spite of their apparent death.

Part Two

★

THE CANYON

MRS. TEMPLE went forward and overtook the leader and walked beside him.

"Mr. Dale," she said, "where are we making for? Phantom Ranch?"

"Phantom Ranch," he said, marching steadily on. The path was very steep now, and he shouted back over his shoulder that the torches might be switched on again. The long crocodile of marchers switched on their tiny lights, making little circles of yellow round their feet. They wound down steadily, making towards the bottom of the canyon. The temperature rose as they went downwards. It became warmer with every step; they passed from a moderate temperature into a semi-tropical. It was odd to drop a mile in altitude more quickly than you would travel eight hundred miles in latitude; odd to fall so quickly on foot, when it would take you so many hours to travel so many horizontal miles, unless, indeed, you travelled in a 'plane.

By the small light of their torches they could see only the path at their feet; they could not see the horrific cliffs around them. This was just as well. The great cliffs might have alarmed them; the path was a path, a safe thing to follow. Most people prefer safe paths to the large unknown. The torches made little rounds of light at their feet. They could see where their footsteps were going. They could not see the larger and more alarming heights above their heads.

They went down; steadily down.

Down into safety.

"Do you remember," said Mrs. Temple, walking beside Mr. Dale, "how people use to take refuge in the Tube stations during the last war?"

Mr. Dale seemed amused by this reminiscence and remarked that he wondered the Americans hadn't run a scenic railway the whole length of the canyon. "Almost as good as a trip through Dante's Inferno," he said.

"Have you thought of the future at all? How long do you suppose we shall remain down here?"

"Does it matter?" he said in a faraway voice. "No, I confess I haven't thought about it yet. One does not know what form this war will take. It may sweep right away from Arizona within a few days. It may rage over our heads for months. It will surely be localized for a time, since much of the American army is here and a great part of their air-force. On the other hand they may fly their air-force away to the defence of their cities; one can't tell."

"The enemy will attack all the cities in turn."

"No: as many as possible at the same time. New York, Chicago, Detroit, Cleveland, Des Moines, Washington, Pittsburg. . . . The American continent never does things by halves; everything is always on the grand scale, whether it is cyclones, earthquakes, railway accidents, or the crashes of big business. The works of God or the works of man. Geographical magnitude seems to affect everything, all through. This war will be no exception. Just you wait and see."

"You make me shudder when you talk about 'this war' in that way. As though you were looking at it through a microscope; as though you had got germs on a slide, crawling about."

"They are not germs," said Mr. Dale; "they are Germans. You do mean a microscope, by the way, don't you, and not a magnifying glass? People are so apt to confuse the two things."

"I do mean a microscope."

"I thought so. I do not know you very well, in fact I have never had any real contact with you until this afternoon, but somehow you struck me at once as a woman who would not make so foolish and inaccurate a confusion. That is meant as a compliment."

"Thank you."

"You are grave, yet humorous. I am glad we are leading this train of people together. It seems strange, does it not, that you and I should have taken control in this way? You must manage the women and I will manage the men."

"I don't know why or how we have arrogated this position to ourselves."

"No. But look. You are walking beside me at the head of this fantastic column. They follow us. They obey us. Why? Simply because we have taken control. People will always obey when they are sufficiently frightened and find somebody to take charge, and since people are so pathetically like children or like sheep, you and I have put ourselves into the position of a nannie or a sheep-dog."

"It sounds a shameful thing to say," said Helen, "when we are on the eve of yet another world-catastrophe, and I will beg you to believe that I am not speaking in any irresponsible spirit. I feel extraordinarily exhilarated. I feel airy, as though I were planing over this war at a great height, almost a stratospheric height, getting those tiny crawlings into a proper perspective. I think this must be the equivalent of your feeling that you are looking through a microscope. A certain unreality lifts me up; my head swims; I realize all the deathly gravity yet I cannot feel cast down. Is it due, do you think, to the vision of courage and self-sacrifice that war brings? The obverse of the medal stamped with horror? The forgetfulness of self in the need to serve a cause? Heroism not heroics."

"I never did set much store by heroism," he said, "if by heroism you mean physical courage. You were speaking of a feeling of exhilaration. Do you not believe that every young airman who takes off for what may be his last flight, his last battle, shares that feeling? Fear is drowned by excitement. There is the sporting instinct, the instinct that makes the racing motorist drive as no man reasonably need, jump horses over fences which could quite easily be passed through a gate, cross waterfalls on tight-ropes, and climb mountain peaks which are useless to you when you do get there. No, give me the man who, like the Prince of Condé, I think it was Condé, looks at himself in the glass on the morning of the battle and says '*Tu trembles, vile carcasse; tu tremblerais bien davantage si tu savais où je vais te mener.*' "

" 'Give me a spirit,' " said Mrs. Temple,

" 'Give me a spirit that on this life's rough sea
   Loves t' have his sails filled with a lusty wind,
   Even till his sail-yards tremble, his masts crack,
   And his rapt ship run on her side so low
   That she drinks water and her keel ploughs air.' "

"I'll cap that for you," said Mr. Dale, who was enjoying himself,

" 'Give me that man that dares bestride
     The active sea-horse, and with pride
     Through that huge field of waters ride;

   'Who with his looks too can appease
     The ruffling winds and raging seas
     In midst of all their outrages.

   'This, this a virtuous man can do,
     Sail against rocks and split them too,
     Ay! and a world of pikes pass through.' "

§

By now it had become very warm, though the party
seemed to be strangely unaffected by the change in
temperature. They marched quietly and without com-
plaint, in a silence broken only by the shuffling of their
feet and an occasional suppressed sob from Madame de
Retz. The first wave of the air attack overhead had passed;
but, looking up the ravine, a red glow from the burning
hotel could be seen in the sky.

"Does that remind you of London? The sky was red
then."

"The sky used to be pink over London, even before
London finally caught fire. There used to be evenings
when the lights of peace blushed the whole heaven. Do
you remember? What nostalgia! As one looked levelly at
twilight across St. James's Park the distance was powder-
blue between the trees, but overhead the sky used to
be lit with the light of millions. Six millions, wasn't it?
or eight, if you included Greater London. About as many
human bodies as Russia and Germany threw in slaughter
against each other."

"Do not think of Russia and Germany now. That
tragedy is over and finished. Do not lament over the
dead. But if you are thinking of London, think now of
New York. When first I saw New York I thought it the
most beautiful and original city in the world. In its own
way. Paris had her beauty, but it was of a recognized
sort, supremely well organized and composed, an example
to all other cities, a triumph of planning and of traditional
architectural elegance. It was possible to compare her
against other capitals to their disadvantage, against
London and even Vienna. Paris stood out as the example
of what all European capitals should be, and were not.
Think of that vista down the Champs-Elysées from the
Arc de Triomphe to the Place de la Concorde; think of

the Rue Royale running up to the Madeleine; think of the Rue de Rivoli with its straight mile of arcades, finer than the street called Straight in Damascus. Think of the Place Vendôme; think of the Louvre and the Tuileries; think of the bridges and the Seine. . . . All so fine and exquisitely composed. Paris represented the peak of European town-planning in the old style. But New York was something different; something new. It was something one had never seen before. Coming to New York for the first time was more like arriving on another planet than arriving in another hemisphere when one was accustomed to western methods and systems. It was startling, this first sight of a city going up high instead of spreading about. You said just now that one looked levelly across St. James's Park. Looking levelly would not apply to New York. In New York one had to look upwards always."

"Yes. I used to wonder what had inspired the architecture of New York. Necessity of course, and the need for providing the maximum of accommodation on the minimum of space. That was obvious. One always accepts the obvious explanation at first, but after I had come to Arizona I began to wonder whether the tremendous geography of this continent hadn't had its influence and suggested these strange upright ideas to the builders of American cities. Streets like canyons,—as near as men could ever get in the reproduction in steel and concrete of the ravine we are descending now.—You were saying just now that geographical magnitude seemed to affect everything all through. Big, bigger, and biggest must be the slogan. That is putting it onto a very material plane. Will you not agree with me that the American mind is constructed in terms of the continent it inhabits? and that the grandeurs and errors of the American mind are commensurate with the area it has had to arrange?"

"I will agree. Americans have to think grandly because

they live grandly. Everything here is on a grand scale. The mistake they made, as you say, is to put everything on to the material plane."

"A vital mistake, but as we all make it let us get back to the discussion we were having. Let us think of coming out of Central Park at twilight, and tell me what you have felt about it."

"One was compelled to look up. One saw oneself faced with a great cliff-face of buildings, open with little rectangles of yellow lights. They are the lights of offices or of flats. They are all lit up. They put the rectangle of their windows into the night like a drop-scene. But it is not in a theatre; it is life. People are living there, working there; one does not know what their lives are, but one can guess. One can make a shot at the common denominator of most lives: the outline is the same, though the details may vary. Anxiety, struggle, competition always; happiness sometimes; discouragement sometimes, then a lift of the spirit, a mood of optimism; a cynical mood, a generous mood; a swaying forwards and backwards like the tide filling and emptying the creeks. The little rock-pools get filled and emptied; their lovely shells of generosity and kindliness get lifted on the swell, then left dry and colourless again. They lie there, exposed to mis-judgement, uncharitableness, and to their own failure to fulfil their own beauty."

"But the tide comes in again, according to your belief: flux and reflux."

"If it were not for that belief I should have put myself out of this world long ago, when everything one cared for seemed to be finished."

"And why didn't you? I often thought of doing so myself. In fact I had provided myself with the means. I was prepared to use them if necessary. I didn't use them. What stopped *you* from doing so? I do not credit or dis-credit you with what are usually called religious scruples."

Mrs. Temple laughed. "Sadie said very much the same thing to me a few hours ago."

"Sadie?"

"The waitress at the hotel. I don't suppose you ever realized her existence. One of the hotel staff to you. Yet she is, or was, a very real person. She is following us now down the trail. She is taking care of the blind man. I have put him in her charge."

"Well, never mind about Sadie—we can leave her to another time. Tell me why you never used your means of putting yourself out of this world, this life. You had no religious faith, you say; no dread that you would lose your immortal soul by rushing it out into another world. So why didn't you use your bare bodkin to your quietus take? What made you shirk the last stab at the last moment?"

"I suppose because the last moment never really arrived. I was an insignificant person, you see, and as a woman past the age of child-bearing I was of no interest to the Germans. After the invasion of England they put me onto a ship with other useless mouths and sent me off. I must say that they had the decency to give me the choice between Australasia, Canada, and America, but I chose the United States. I already knew the States,—I had lived there,—I knew and loved Arizona,—I had travelled over much of the world and had come to the conclusion that Arizona was one of the most beautiful regions I had ever seen—even as you were saying just now that New York was one of the most beautiful of cities. So I came here to Arizona. As well here as anywhere else."

"And decided to go on living."

"May I turn the tables on you? You're English too; you must have had the same decision to take; you evidently took the same decision as I did. Why?"

"Well, it seemed a very curious and interesting thing, to take the other decision,—the decision to die. In desperation, yes, but in cold blood? Think of it in detail. One would lay oneself down in an orderly way on a couch or a bed, having attired oneself suitably first, if one had the time to do so,—pyjamas or a nightshirt or a silken nightgown,—it seems more proper to die in night attire, I can't think why. That is not the point. The point is that it should be an interesting decision to take, to kill oneself. Why should it be so interesting? or, indeed, interesting at all? Philosophically, it should be a small fact to step over from this life into another one. Every fisherman knows that you put your foot onto a stepping-stone and jump the stream on to the other bank. Then why do we hesitate? Why did we hesitate, you and I? It wasn't cowardice surely? not cowardice in the accepted sense? No. It was something deeper than that. It was the reluctance to leave the life we knew for the life we did not know; the old story. Old stories have a way of being true stories. There is a thing which might be known as the reluctance to die by one's own hand. I will admit to you, Mrs. Temple, that I hesitated too long to take those little tablets out of their little bottle. I knew they would kill me, swiftly and painlessly. I hated the idea of pain but I thought I did not mind the idea of death. I found, when it came to the point of decision, that I minded the idea of death also. I found that I couldn't put myself out of this life by my own volition."

"The point of decision was too sharp for you? It was too like running yourself onto the tip of a bayonet? Bayonets are very sharp. I had to watch my dog being stuck by a bayonet during the last war. That was worse than taking painless tablets for myself.—I do not know why I tell you things like these. A candour has come over me which I cannot explain. I have never told these things to any living person before. I do not know why I tell you these things now."

"I do not know either. Usually, people tell these things

only when they love. Lover reveals to lover; and that is the supreme egotistical indulgence of love. But you and I, Mrs. Temple, are not lovers; never have been; and never will be."

"We have never been even acquaintances until to-day."

"Such things grow rapidly when war comes. As it happens, I started to watch you this afternoon, some hours before this trouble began. I had no idea then that another war was about to break over us. I was amusing myself by observing you as a fellow-guest. I had no idea, then, that we should see the hotel in flames, Royer killed, and ourselves taking refuge in the canyon. You didn't know I was watching you this afternoon. You were talking to one of the Indian boys; you were sending him off on a message. You were sending him off into the Painted Desert—to whom? To the hermit?"

"And what made you imagine that I should be sending a message to the hermit? A short time ago you seemed never to have heard of him."

"True. I had not. I know now."

"Someone spoke to you of him?"

"No. I *know*. I cannot tell you how I know. I just know."

"I have no friends, Mr. Dale. The hermit was a mere acquaintance left over from the old Europe. I liked and enjoyed the strength of his mind and I think he tolerated me here in Arizona because I never bothered him. I left him to himself. Certain persons like the hermit prefer being left to themselves. He stayed alone in his cave, and occasionally he allowed me to visit him there. He was always very courteous and entertaining, but I think he welcomed me only because he knew I should not stay too long."

"It is rather ironical that he and some others should have abandoned England so early in the belief that

America offered the only hope of a surviving civilization.
I wonder what they think now?"

Mrs. Temple made no reply. No reply seemed necessary.

§

They trudged on. They went downwards and downwards. The climate became warmer and even warmer,
but it still did not seem to affect those who were going
down into it.

They trudged on.

"Are you tired?"

"No, oddly enough, I am not. I feel as though I should
never be tired again."

"Or ill?"

"Or ill."

"Have you ever been very ill?"

"Well, I have had operations."

"And suffered?"

"One can't have operations without suffering, can
one?"

"So you know what pain is?"

"I think I may say that I know what pain is. But I
don't like to speak of it. One doesn't like to speak of so
private a thing; one keeps that sort of thing to oneself,
after it is over."

"Of course. But we are living in such a reality now
that I had no hesitation in forcing you to speak. We
spend far too much of our lives trying not to reveal ourselves to one another. Why? Such a waste of time. As you
were saying just now, one can make a shot at the common
denominator of most lives, which really means that we
all know the essential things about one another although
we take so much trouble to conceal them. Even dictators,
my dear Mrs. Temple, must sometimes lie in their baths
contemplating their white vulnerable bodies, grotesque

and absurd. Does Hitler, when he lies soaking in his bath, ever wonder about the bullet piercing his own belly? The belly of Hitler, that container of digestive organs, coils of intestines, that sack of complicated contraptions, that bag of guts, as readily burst and exuding as the belly of any poor old cab-horse lifted on the horns in a bull-fight; that target of every assassin, that symbol of collective revenge. . . . Does Hitler think on these things, as he lies in his bath, stripped, naked, and alone?"

§

They reached the bottom of the trail and arrived at Phantom Ranch. Here the whole procession halted. The neat little encampment loomed before them, but no one seemed inclined to take advantage of its hospitality. No one seemed inclined to open the door and go inside, to throw themselves down in exhaustion on the couches: they all seemed content to remain outside in the warm night air, strolling vaguely and happily in the softness of the bottom of the canyon. The river rushed and echoed among its rocks. They thought about Echo Cave; Echo Cave reverberated with strange sounds, but no stranger than the sounds that Mr. Dale now switched on from the radio set of Phantom Ranch. America had come onto the air again. But in an unusual fashion. It was only after much twisting of the pointer that the voice came through with any clarity:

". . . in successive waves sweeping down from the Canadian border.—Telephonic communication with New York has been interrupted and it is impossible at present to discover what is happening in the city.—Radio service will be maintained continuously for as long as possible on wave-length G7563 and emergency wave-length F8970 (G for Georgia, F for Florida); we regret that our

usual transmitting stations are temporarily out of action.—
Stand by. Stand by. Another bulletin is just coming
through. Stand by. Hold on. In one minute's time we
will give you the new bulletin.—Are you there? This is
the National Broadcasting Company calling on wave-
length G7563 and also on emergency wave-length F8970.
This is the N.B.C. calling the United States of America.
A state of national emergency has been declared from
the White House, but all communication with the White
House has now been interrupted. We are at present
unable to explain why communication with Washington
should have been interrupted. We hope to resume contact
later on.—Telephonic communication is interrupted all
over the country.—Sabotage is suspected.—Do not
attempt to contact your friends and relations by telephone.
You will be doing a bad service to your country. Keep
quiet wherever you are. Do not panic. Stay where you
are. Remember the crowded roads of Europe. Crowded
by refugees. Do not repeat that mistake.—Stand by
again; Stand by. Two minutes' delay."

The whole miscellaneous party wandered vaguely
round the buildings of Phantom Ranch, waiting for the
voice to come again through the opened windows and
the opened door. Mr. Dale had thrown everything open,
so that the voice might come out into the night. The little
party was at the very bottom of the Canyon now. They
listened, but only with half their minds; the other half
was floating away on ideas of their own. The realism of
what was happening in the outside other world affected
them only at a second remove.

The radio voice came through again.

"Here is America calling the United States of America.
Hallo, America. We are glad to inform you that the N.B.C.
has now been able to arrange with the still friendly
Republic of the Argentine for the N.B.C. programmes to
be transmitted from Buenos Aires. All N.B.C. stations
except G7563 and F8970 are now off the air, and we

I

cannot guarantee that those stations will not also be off
the air during the next twenty-four hours. So if you
cannot get our programme, tune in to Buenos Aires.—
Stand by again; stand by. America calling. N.B.C.
America calling. Stand by; stand by. One moment,
please."

"We have to report that during the past three hours
enemy attacks have been launched in many parts of the
continent. So far as can be ascertained no enemy land-
troops have crossed either the Canadian or the Mexican
frontiers, but air-borne troops are reported to have been
landed at various points in the Middle West, notably at
St. Louis, Missouri; Des Moines, Iowa; Indianapolis,
Indiana; Springfield, Illlinois. It is not possible at present
to determine what is taking place in these areas. It is
known however that German warships have appeared
off the coast of Maine and it is believed that a naval
action is now in progress. It is known also that large
enemy air detachments have appeared over Detroit,
Chicago, Pittsburgh, Pennsylvania (not Pittsburgh,
Kansas, or Pittsburg, Kentucky, or Pittsburg, Texas),
and it is feared also over Washington, D.C., and New
York. This may explain why communication with the
capital and with New York is temporarily interrupted.
We trust that the interruption may be temporary only
and will be presently resumed.—Now to fill the pause
before our next bulletin here is a gramophone record.
Land of Hope and Glory."

"They don't know about *us*, evidently," said Mr. Dale.
"Not a word about poor Arizona. When do you suppose
the air-borne troops will arrive here?"

"They are almost bound to arrive, unless you think
they intend to destroy all this section of the American
army by air-attack first."

"That is probably their idea; but remember that all
this section of the American Air Force will go up to meet
them and such a battle will be fought over the Painted

Desert as the desert has never seen before. It will be enough to draw the fossils from their rocks."

"It seems rash, doesn't it, to have brought so much of the air-force and the army for their manœuvres so near to Mexico where the Nazis were known to be in control?"

Mr. Dale laughed. He laughed as though he really enjoyed the joke.

"My dear lady, you forget that after the assassination of the late President Roosevelt, a Treaty of Agreement and Co-operation was entered into between the Government of the United States and the Government of the Third Reich. I am quite prepared to believe that the present President was acting according to his best beliefs when he affixed his signature at the bottom of that disastrous document.

> Chimborazo, Cotopaxi
> Had stolen his heart away.

That wouldn't have mattered. By all means let his heart be stolen by two dormant Mexican volcanoes. No one would have minded that. What did matter was that the Nazis stole away with his aerodromes in Sonora and Chihuahua. That is what we are paying for in Arizona now. They are only just over the border and we have already had some cause to realize it."

"It does not seem to matter to us down here. Selfishly it does not seem to matter. Is it because we have arrived at Phantom Ranch? Is it because we are safe at the bottom of the canyon removed from all material danger?"

The whole party was humming *Land of Hope and Glory* now, a subdued and singularly harmonious choir. It was surprising to find that that heterogeneous company had so much music in its collective soul.

§

Overhead the bombers came again. Fighters came with them, and the needle of machine-guns threaded the pauses between the explosions of the big bombs. They were trying to hit the camp, guided by the flames from the hotel.

"Royer has done his work well," said Dale grimly. "That funeral pyre of our Manager will mean the death of thousands as well as the loss of his own miserable life. The camp is a small concentrated town of huts and tents, a grand target for to-night. Our beautiful desert, a Persian carpet stained with the colours of Nature and strewn with the rocks of ages, will be stained with the blood of men and strewn with the bones of men when the sun next rises over it. *El desierto pintado*, the Spaniards called it with remarkable felicity.—I wonder how long it will be before the N.B.C. tells us what is happening here in the south-west. *Land of Hope and Glory*, indeed! Land of despair and shame."

"Sunrise cannot be far off. Look up. What is that light in the sky? Is it the light of the sun or the light of fires, the light of life or the incandescence of death?"

"Both, I think. In a few minutes the sun will be up over the horizon, making the fires pale. The colours of the desert will come to life again, with the staining meres of blood added to them. Do you think they will be squelchy underfoot, those patches of good American blood? If you walked across them, would your feet sink in and your shoes fill with a pink and slimy soup, or would the rock be too hard underneath them?"

"Look up again. The sky is no longer only black and red; there are streaks of lemon; I think sunrise must be coming."

"It will take some time before the light reaches us down here; we shall have to wait until the sun is directly overhead. There is warmth at the bottom of the canyon, but there is darkness too. Light will stream over America, but it will be a light revealing things that America will not like. It will show ruin and a distraught people; things that America has never known. She will have to get used to them. She will not enjoy the process. She will now have to learn to endure the things that Czechoslovakia, Poland, Greece, Belgium, France, Holland, Russia, Britain endured. She will see her cities destroyed and her little villages too. She will see not only New York, Washington, Boston and 'Frisco destroyed, but also Shenandoah in Virginia, Pigeonroost in Kentucky, Rome, Athens and Vienna in Georgia. Small homesteads in Texas and Nebraska will be attacked, even as Ipswich, Canterbury and Sutton Valence were attacked and taken in the last war, and little farmsteads seized in Essex and Devon,—all over England in that surprising way. We in England began to understand war when the war-communiqués began to record familiar humble names. We had never understood it until then. Perhaps it is only now that the Americans will begin to understand it. They will be surprised when the planes swoop down, spraying the roofs of their barns with machine-gun bullets, and the air-borne troops come down on the little harmless farms. European farmers got themselves accustomed to that, but American farmers have not accustomed themselves to it; not yet. I daresay they will adapt themselves to it in time. One adapts oneself in due time to every exaction of war. One's standards alter very quickly, once war comes. One very soon adapts oneself to living in a ditch instead of in a house. This is a truth which we have learnt but which the Americans have yet to learn."

§

Daylight began overhead. Looking up, they saw pale yellow bars across the sky. The shadows in the canyon deepened, although no light came down there yet. It was very beautiful down there, looking upwards at that hour of dawn. The level sun sent horizontal shadows along the rocks and startled the tips into colour; the tips of the rocks in that early sunlight were as rosy, as delicate, as the nipples of a woman's breast. They stood up, mountain high. Gradually as the sun rose higher, streaks of sunlight like the sticks of an inverted fan began to descend into the ravine, touching the lower strata of the rocks with colour until the colour grew and grew, swarming over all the rocks, swarming, creeping, growing into a symphony of colour which seemed to combine with music and with truth.

§

"Dear me," said Mr. Dale, "the radio is coming on again. I suppose we'd better listen."

They listened.

"This is America calling from Buenos Aires. This is America calling the United States from Buenos Aires. We have to announce that enemy attacks are developing all over the North-American continent. We regret to announce that two cruisers and two destroyers have been sunk in the naval engagement off the coast of Maine, previously reported. The next-of-kin will be informed as soon as possible. Two destroyers of the enemy fleet are known to have been sunk; two cruisers are believed to have been damaged.—This is America calling the United States of North America from Buenos Aires. We have information now that a serious air-attack has developed over the Grand Canyon of the Colorado region in Arizona where heavy bombing is taking place over troop-concentration camps and air-drome hangars in this region. We have no exact information as to what is taking place in this region but hope to report later in further detail.—Hold on, please. One moment, please."

The voice paused.

The voice resumed:

"We regret also to announce that a more serious air-attack has recently developed over New York City. We are at present unable to state what the damage to New York may be. Enemy submarines also appear to have made their way into the harbour off Manhattan and it seems likely that one of them has exploded a mine, doing considerable damage which may possibly involve the destruction of the Statue of Liberty. This is not certain yet; we hope for later reports contradicting so regrettable an incident."

§

The dawn grew. The shadows deepened and blackened as the sunlight came down. Finally morning came. The air-battles overhead had ceased. The wickedness of the night gave place to the loveliness of day. The blind man came towards Mrs. Temple, walking freely.

She put out her hand towards him, to help him on his way. She thought he might stumble, but he did not stumble.

"Good morning, Mrs. Temple. What a lovely morning it is. How beautiful the rocks are, when one looks up at them from this angle. The early sunlight on them . . . . How it slopes down gradually, putting huge shadows on some places and then bright light on other places. What a gift of God, to see light and shadows like that."

"I thought you were blind," she said.

"I was."

§

Sadie came to her later in the morning.

"Mrs. Temple, dear. You told me to call you that way."

"Yes, Sadie, what?"

"You know you put me in charge of that blind man?"

"Yes, Sadie, so I did."

"Well, he sees now."

"Yes, I know he does."

"Odd, isn't it? I can't think why. It seems a miracle. Very odd it seems to me."

"Very odd. Odd things do happen down here."

"He sees now. He sees as well as you or I do. So I don't need to lead him about any more, do I?"

"No, Sadie, you don't; but thank you for having led him down so far."

"Mrs. Temple, dear, there is another thing I want to tell you."

"Yes, Sadie, what?"

"I've lost my cough."

"Lost your cough?"

"Yes, I used to spit blood, you know. I used to cough my chest out, every morning, and cough blood up with it. I used to stain three handkerchiefs a day. I used to wash them out in the sink so that nobody else should see them. I was afraid of getting sent away."

"Sent away?"

"Yes. Mr. Royer,—I don't like to say anything against him now. He's dead, isn't he? He died up there, in the hotel, last night. Was it only last night? It seems ages ago. Anyhow, I was saying, I was afraid of getting sent away by Mr. Royer. It would have given a bad name to the hotel if anybody knew there was a consumptive waitress there. He was kind to me in a way, he kept me on when he might have fired me. It's true he did cut my wages down because he said I wasn't worth the money I was getting,—you see I did have to take a few hours off sometimes when I got that cough,—but still he did keep me on, and I was grateful for that. But all that is past and now I feel as though I had never been ill. I suppose the climate down here suits me. I suppose I ought to feel that the things that are happening now are far more terrible than anything which could ever have happened to me, but somehow nothing seems real, only very exciting and magnificent. I daresay it is just because I can't take it all in."

Helen looked at the girl. Her cheeks had lost their pallor; the anxious careworn expression had left her eyes; she no longer looked like a dog that expects to be beaten. She stood upright, happy with confidence, an altered being.

§

The sun was up now. He was riding high. The people down at Phantom Ranch felt the warmth of his beams. He seemed to have sent the evil of the night attack away, and to have restored some sanity with daylight to a civilized world. Yet that was a delusion. Insanity was still travelling about.

"Here is America calling from Buenos Aires by courtesy of the Argentine Republic. Calling the United States of America. Calling all Europe, Asia, Africa and Australia. Calling the world. Enemy attacks have continued throughout the night and it now seems fairly certain that at some points the air-borne troops of the enemy are established in temporary possession. It is confidently expected, however, that these occupying forces will be disposed of before many days have elapsed. It is feared that destruction on several cities has been extensive and that a heavy casualty list must be anticipated. We record these reports, not in order to spread alarm, but in pursuance of a request from the White House before communication was interrupted that radio reporting should be as accurate as possible. This request was telephonically promulgated to the N.B.C. by the President's Private Secretary, but we are unable to state whether he was acting on his own initiative or on the President's orders. It was found impossible to discover the whereabouts of the President; it is believed that he took off from Washington by plane during the earlier part of yesterday afternoon, piloting himself, for an unknown destination. The naval action earlier reported off the coast of Maine . . ."

Here the voice faded out.

Everybody seemed relieved that the obligation to listen should be removed. They dispersed vaguely but happily to make some stray arrangements for themselves in the little encampment of Phantom Ranch. Their requirements were few and it seemed to matter little to them whether they spent the day and the following nights in shelter or in the open. Some of them lay down on a ledge of rock and slept like animals in the shade away from the sun. Others went and amused themselves with the echoes; it was said that you could get eight repeated echoes from a single rifle-shot; it was said that you could hear an Indian singing on the other rim of the canyon and yet be unable to make yourself heard by a person a few yards off. This mode of existence suited the company down at the bottom of the canyon.

Towards midday when the sun was high an Indian boy came and perched himself on the Rim and called down into the deeps. He knew exactly how to manage the echoes and how to send his voice. The radio from Buenos Aires was still silent, but the primitive science of the Indian was independent of scientific contraptions. Putting his hands to his mouth he called down to Mrs. Temple:

"Madam! Madam! Mrs. Temple! Message from Mr. Hermit: Message from Mr. Alden. He alive still. He sends love. He all right. He say not trouble about war. He say not trouble about him. He say not trouble about anything. He say everything all right in the end. He sends love."

The last word wandered round and round the gorges: Love, love, love, love. . . . The echoes gradually faded

out as the radio of war-news had faded out; but as the
last echo died away a rifle-shot was heard on the Rim
and the body fell bouncing from cliff to cliff, to land
broken at Mrs. Temple's feet.

She bent over him.

"Poor boy, he has carried his last message for the
hermit. He was a good boy and faithful. They must have
snipers up there on the Rim."

The boy opened his eyes and smiled up at her.

"Mr. Hermit all right."

"Yes," she said; "don't worry; we are all perfectly
all right."

§

"Do you know," said Mr. Dale, coming up to her some
hours later, "the first time I saw you talking to that
Indian boy I thought what a romantic couple you made.
It was, dear me, only yesterday afternoon. It seems much
longer ago, but with a curious telescoping of time or an
equally curious inversion of time it might be a thousand
years ago or it might not be going to happen until
to-morrow. That sounds rather like Alice-through-the-
looking-glass, but it is the kind of thing that has always
interested me in my amateurish way. Living down here
seems to upset one's sense of time. I do not think that any
of us have quite adjusted our sense of time down here yet.
I do not think that any of us have quite adjusted our sense
of anything that we used to regard as important in the
old life up on the Rim. There are snipers up on the Rim.
There are no snipers down here. There are bombers up
over the Painted Desert. Bombs cannot reach us down here.
Hunger does not seem to trouble us, nor thirst. If I were
a sentimentalist, which I never was and shall not now
become, I should remark that Phantom Ranch seems
made of flowers and running water and goodwill."

Madame de Retz joined them, smiling broadly.

"I bring something to entertain you. It is all that I have left of my possessions; I ran upstairs for my bird last night when the fire started and I snatch this at the same time. It represented my livelihood, you understand. I had many of them, but only two could I carry. The other one I dropped on my flight and even this one—see—is charred." She showed them the big ledger, with the cover half torn off and some pages blackened. "Look and read," she said handing it to Mrs. Temple. "It was my bible once; my fortune. It seems foolish now."

"But this is fascinating," Helen exclaimed. "Look, Mr. Dale. Here is the index, so neatly written out; it seems to contain the names of every celebrity you have ever heard of ("and a great many more you have not," Madame de Retz interjected with pride). See, here are the cross-references: Theatre, films, race-going, royalty, beauty, divorce, social, political . . . what on earth does it all mean, madame?"

"I explain. It is my life-work as well as my livelihood. I am proud. You wonder why it is not in Polish. I have to keep it in English because my employers are American and I send a duplicate always to New York. It is very secret, very secret indeed. If the New York office is not bombed, then my duplicate will still exist and my life-work will not be lost. Twenty volumes I had, a real encyclopaedia cosmopolitan, and they blow now all over the Painted Desert."

The two English people were sure by now that they had come on an elaborate plot which Madame de Retz was revealing to them, impelled by some strange bravado. They were interested to observe the methods by which the Nazi agents had worked, although it was unfortunately too late to do anything about it and although they were shocked by the fact that Madame de Retz whose own country had suffered so violently under the German attack should sell herself in the cause of German propaganda. They felt quite detached about it, however, and even had a certain sympathy with a poor woman who had her living to earn: the instinct of personal preservation has always been strong. Who could tell? perhaps she had been blackmailed into this treachery.

They sat side by side on a boulder and peered obediently into the big pages as Madame de Retz pointed with her finger at the various entries.

"You see, here you have the name in the first column. Alphabetical, of course. Surname and first name,—what you English call Christian name. Block letters. Neat! yes? Then next column: Occupation. Next column: Special Qualifications. Next column: Value in dollars. You notice, divorce ranks high. Every divorce adds a possible thousand dollars to the price, because every re-marriage means extra sex-appeal of course. Titled-divorce and celebrity-divorce come separate. Titles were good once, then a slump in title-value, then they came up again. It is difficult to explain the reason for these things. Once," she said with a chuckle of real pleasure, "I got a Brazilian with eight divorces and seven re-marriages. That was my record. Oh, I was proud. My committee congratulated me. They thought me a very good agent. But Royalty was always better than divorce, perhaps because more difficult to persuade. You do not know how haughty Royalty can be, turning up its nose. I had a nice little scheme prepared here. I had begun to approach your little friend Miss Driscoll for her colleague Princess Irma; the child seemed shy, but I knew how to manage that, and in a few days, a very few days, I think I should win her round. The young are very easy to twist round the little finger. Now I suppose it is too late, and although the time for my work seems to be past I am still a little sorry. Ah well, I must not regret. She was not a real

Royal Highness, it is true, but only a Balkan one, and the Balkan ones were never first-class in value."

"But I still don't quite understand," Mrs. Temple began. "What would this . . . this miscellaneous collection of people do for you? I notice that most of them are women. The men are nearly all actors . . . or film stars. . . ."

"Ah, that is for the make-up," cried Madame de Retz excitedly. "That is high value and the men were very good-natured always. Very easy to obtain. 'Anything to oblige you, madame,' they would say, 'anything to do you a good turn,' and although I always thanked them and said how kind you are to a poor woman, I knew they thought of the publicity value to them. Publicity never comes amiss, was a slogan of my committee. But never mind about the men; I snap my fingers at them really. No, I will confide to you my greatest ambition. Ah, it was my mad, my secret dream; it was so mad, so secret, I told not even my committee. I dreamt one day I would present my committee with a *fait accompli*. I would travel to New York in person; I would demand to be received at a board meeting; I would appear before all those gentlemen; I would throw the document on the table before the Chairman; I would not speak; I would let the document speak for me."

She drew herself up and threw her hand out in a dramatic gesture. Helen and Mr. Dale gazed at her; they were more puzzled than ever and wondered whether the woman was dangerous, inspired, or merely insane.

"I show you," she whispered, and bending down she turned over the pages of the index, running her fingers down the column until she came to the letter E. "Look, I put it in pencil for myself only," she said; "I do not copy this entry into the duplicate for my committee. Only when I have achieved my ambition will I reveal it."

She pointed. "ENGLAND, QUEEN OF. What do you say to that?"

"Good God," said Mr. Dale, who was not easily startled. "You didn't seriously suppose that you could inveigle the Queen into your Quisling intrigues,—the *Queen*? I don't think we ought to listen to this, Mrs. Temple. It seems almost treasonable. Let us leave this mad woman to her ravings."

Madame de Retz stared at him; she looked dismayed and as though she were about to cry.

"Quisling?" she repeated. "Treasonable? Oh no! Foolish perhaps, and indeed it all looks foolish now to me, but believe me I have the highest respect for Her Majesty,—it was a foolish dream,—I should not have told you,—but we all have our ambitions and you must not mock me. This was mine. If I could secure your Queen. . . ."

Mrs. Temple saw that there was some misunderstanding.

"Tell me," she said gently, as one speaks to a frightened child, "what exactly did you want of the Queen?"

"Only her name, I promise you; I would not ask her to *use* the stuff; only ask her to allow me to *say* she used it. Our fortune would be made,—my fortune would be made."

"Stuff? What stuff?"

"Our face-cream, Mrs. Temple; our beauty preparation. World famous. All film-stars, all professional beauties use it. One application overnight and the result is magical. We pay good prices, I promise you, for the advertisement. My committee, for instance, would pay five hundred dollars, one hundred pounds sterling, to your little friend Miss Driscoll if she got Princess Irma's signature; and then fifteen hundred dollars, five hundred pounds to Princess Irma herself. You see? Commission! What would we pay to the person who secured the Queen of England for us? Any fortune, any day! and a little fortune to this poor Polish agent, Wilmushka de Retz, your humble servant."

She made a funny facetious yet graceful little curtsey as she ended her speech; she curtsied to Mrs. Temple and Mr. Dale as they sat on their boulder studying her large ledger, her life work, her dossier; and Mr. Dale, after peering first into the pages and then looking up at Madame de Retz, was inclined to break into laughter, but there was something so serious and touching in her aspect that he could not laugh at her but said, "Do go on, madame, Tell us more. I never knew until now how these things were worked."

Madame de Retz brightened; she was sensitive enough to have felt the chill of their disapproval, but now that she had regained their sympathy and interest she was eager to tell them anything she could.

"I planned to offer Her Majesty a little outfit, a box containing all the preparations from A to Z. The box should have the Royal Arms engraved on it, very pretty, ivory with black engraving and black hinges, I designed it myself, very compact and convenient for travelling. . . ."

"I thought you said you didn't want her to use the stuff; only to lend her name to it."

"It was good stuff," said Madame de Retz earnestly, "it would do no harm, but I would be content for the little outfit to be put on Her Majesty's dressing-table. Now I tell you about A to Z, shall I?"

"Please do."

She was delighted; she clapped her hands together, the hands that Loraine Driscoll had compared to claws.

"It was my own idea. A clever idea, I think; my committee congratulated me again. We had twenty-six preparations, so I made an alphabet, one letter to each." She started to rattle it off by heart, checking on her fingers. "A—Apple Cheek, B—Beauty cream, C—Carnation, D—Debutante, E—Eternal love, F—Fidelity,

G—Good luck, H—Here we are again! I—It's me!
J—Jolly girl, K—Kiss me, L—Love me, M—Miss me,
N—Night of love, O—Open door, P—Please don't!
Q—Queen of Hearts, R—Royal approval, S—Sovereign
Solution, T—*Toujours à toi*, U—Useful always, V—
. . . — (she tapped it out) V Victory, W—Woo me, win
me, X—Excellent, Y—Youthful blush, Z—z was diffi-
cult."

"And what did you find for Z? Zebra and zig-zag
would both be too stripy for any woman's complexion;
zeitgist would be unpopular as a German word in occupied Europe; zebu . . .' "

"Mr. Dale, I fear you laugh at me. What did I find?
I found Zephyr. I thought that was pretty. It suggests
the breeze blowing colour into a woman's cheeks. Very
rural, very country tint, popular in England specially. It
came well at the end of the list after Y—Youthful blush.
Z—Zephyr."

"Madame, you are an artist, I see."

"You flatter me, Mr. Dale. My committee think so
too, 'An artist at your job,' they say, 'and practical as
well.' That was their letter. I was proud."

"I don't wonder," said Mrs. Temple, who was rather
touched by this mixture of absurdity and enthusiasm. "I
can't imagine how you devise these things. You must have
a very lively mind. I am sure your committee must regard
you as invaluable."

Madame de Retz began suddenly to giggle. Under the
warmth of their approval she became coy. "Oh, you are
both too kind. Your kindness encourages me to confide
in you something about my alphabet. Not only Z was
difficult. All the letters were difficult. They suggest things
called improper. It is a pity, because they are things that
suit beauty preparations. Great scope for risky joke.
Perhaps you English do not understand. I see my confidence does not go well with you. I will go away from you

K

now, and you will say that Polish woman has a nasty mind. You will condemn me, but I will go away alone by myself up the creek and leave you to condemn me. I go without my Grigori."

She went, a lonely little figure, wandering away.

"May God forgive me," said Mr. Dale, "after our experience of Royer I had begun to think her ledger might have something to do with the Gestapo. Poor innocent! Poor silly innocent! How one does misjudge people, to be sure. Let us hope that we may learn some wisdom, down here."

§

It had never fallen to the lot of any member of the party to wander untrammelled in the mysterious depths of the canyon as they wandered now during the days that followed. Although many of them had made the descent, and had even spent a couple of nights at Phantom Ranch, they had always been accompanied by guides whom it was impossible to shake off and whose raucous descriptions and explanations had pursued them into creeks and caverns where no sound should have been allowed to penetrate but the roar of the rapids or the brushing of the wings of a bird. Now they were free to come and go as they pleased, with a chosen companion or alone if the desire for solitude took them. Disaster after disaster was recorded from the outside world, but down here dwelt the peace and beauty of the Elysian Fields, and a harmony of sight and sound to which was matched an incomparable fantasy of Nature. Intimacy came with the prolonged acquaintance, yet no true intimacy was possible with the moods successively imposed. Was it storm? then the cliffs darkened above the abyss and their shapes were lost in sombrous masses overhead. Was it rain? then all the waterfalls fell like treble voices into the

bass of the river and rainbows stood from pinnacle to
pinnacle, not only rainbows which bridged the chasm
from rim to rim, but miniature iridescences also which
danced over the spray of every falling splash. Was it a
day of clouds? then they rolled from peak to peak, some
crags so sharp that it seemed their spikes must pierce
the roundness of the cloud and explode it into a revelation
of the blue heaven beyond. Was it sunset? then the rocks
became as fossilized wine, claret hardened into cathe-
drals, great ships breasting forward, with the shadows
like the trough of the wave and these edifices riding still
sunlit above them. No comparison could be too extravagant, for the scale was so huge it seemed made to match
the scale of catastrophe going on in the outside world,
with the difference that here was the exaggeration of
natural splendour in contrast to the small ingenious folly
of twentieth-century man.

> House made of the dawn,
> House made of evening light,
> House made of the dark cloud,
> House made of male rain,
> House made of dark mist,
> House made of female rain,
> House made of pollen,
> House made of grasshoppers.
> Dark cloud is at the door.
> The trail of it is dark cloud,
> The zigzag lightning stands high up on it.

> Being as it used to be long ago, may I walk,
> May it be happy before me,
> May it be beautiful behind me,
> May it be beautiful below me,
> May it be beautiful above me,
> May it be beautiful, all around me,
> In beauty it is finished.

Man the inheritor of such a planet. . . . Those who wandered at their leisure about the Grand Canyon of the Colorado during those days of battle between the Reich-controlled States of Europe and the Federated States of North America, went back in their imagination to the men who had first come upon that region.—There was a time when the canyon had never been seen by the white man. Don Lopez de Cardeñas, travelling with twelve other Spaniards in 1540 in search of "seven cities of gold," came upon it without any warning. They were the most astonished men on earth that day. It is surprising enough to stand for the first time upon the Rim when you know more or less what to expect, an experience for which no description can be a sufficient preparation, but to ride for days across the desert with no idea of what lies ahead, and then to come to a halt so sudden that it throws your horse back on his haunches as the earth splits into that gash,—there, *there* would be a moment of history worth attending.

The Spanish adventurers tried to find a way down to the river but the trackless cliffs defeated them, and for another two hundred years the canyon returned to its solitude. Indians prowled fearfully along the rims; blue jays flashed like kingfishers between the rocks; the cascades fell with every rain; but no white man came to look at that place again until two Franciscan friars crossed the river at a ford thereafter called *El vado de los Padres.*

A hundred years later a man with only one arm went down the river by boat. It was the first time that either the red man or the white had travelled that river; the first time that any human eye had contemplated those appalling steeps from the bottom. Men had looked down upon them from the top, seeing them as inverted mountains, seeing the peak instead of the base; but this man and his companions saw the Colorado and the canyon it had cut, from the bottom instead of from the top. They had no idea where they were going or what lay ahead. They woke echoes in caves that had never given back the human voice, and sang or spoke to one another, scarcely able to believe that their own words were returning to them, so transformed were the tones by some soft resonance of the rock. They gave names to unnamed places,— Music Temple, Marble Canyon, Vermilion Cliffs, Flaming Gorge, Split Mountain, Bright Angel River,—leaving behind them this trail of imaginative names which, far from exceeding, could scarcely represent the reality. That was all behind them; but as they let down their boats over rapid after rapid, happy if they could make a few miles in calmer waters during the day and find a camping place as darkness fell, they still knew nothing of what they were coming to. The future lay unknown as the future of life with its only certainty of death, and indeed it seemed probable that this journey would end in the same way. For hundreds of miles they had surmounted dangers, but there might be hundreds of miles ahead with insurmountable dangers; they could not estimate how many miles or what dangers; rapids they could not descend, impassable passages, mountain sides closing in on them in too narrow a fissure: from such difficulties there would be no return. They might just succeed in making their way down the stream, but they could never come back against it. You can shoot your boat down a rapid, but you cannot retrace. Still the man with one arm went on and came eventually at midday into a calm valley he could geographically recognize. The relief from danger, he wrote, and the joy of success were great, and his joy was almost ecstasy.

"We have looked back unnumbered centuries into the past, and seen the time when the schists in the depths of the Grand Cañon were first formed as sedimentary beds beneath the sea; we have seen this long period followed by another of dry land—so long that even hundreds, or perhaps thousands, of feet of beds were washed away by the rains; and, in turn, followed by another period of ocean triumph, so long, that at least ten thousand feet of sandstones were accumulated as sediments, when the sea yielded dominion to the powers of the air, and the region was again dry land. But aerial forces carried away the ten thousand feet of rocks, by a process slow yet unrelenting, until the sea again rolled over the land, and more than ten thousand feet of rocky beds were built over the bottom of the sea; and then again the restless sea retired, and the golden, purple, and black hosts of heaven made missiles of their own misty bodies—balls of hail, flakes of snow, and drops of rain—and when the storm of war came, the new rocks fled to the sea. Now we have cañon gorges and deeply eroded valleys, and still the hills are disappearing, the mountains themselves are wasting away, the plateaus are dissolving and the geologist, in the light of the past history of the earth, makes prophecy of a time when this desolate land of Titanic rocks shall become a valley of many valleys, and yet again the sea will invade the land, and the coral animals build their reefs in the infinitesimal laboratories of life, and lowly beings shall weave nacre-lined shrouds for themselves, and the shrouds shall remain entombed in the bottom of the sea; when the people shall be changed, by the chemistry of life, into new forms; monsters of the deep shall live and die, and their bones be buried in the coral sands. Then other mountains and other hills shall be washed into the Colorado Sea, and coral reefs, and shales, and bones, and disintegrated mountains, shall be made into beds of rock, for a new land, where new rivers shall flow."

§

On the fifth day a young man fell into the Canyon with his plane. He fell as the Indian boy had fallen, crashing from rock to rock; but it was not only his own soft body that crashed, it was the fabric of the plane, the wings,

the fuselage, the cabin, all smashing and splintering with
the noise that a plane makes when it breaks up, a noise
disproportionate to so dragon-fly a thing. Only those
who had already heard it happen could recognize so
particular a noise, but even they had heard it only in open
country or at most in the streets of a town; they had
never heard so strange a reverberation as that which woke
those stony echoes and ran up the ravines and returned
to break again upon opposite walls and die away in
further recesses until silence was left to be filled by the
roaring river once more.

The fall had been as beautiful as the fall of a shot bird;
sudden as a plummet from the sky, the plane had hit the
Rim and bounded out to strike the first crag and then
to drop with one shattered wing between hundreds of
feet of precipice, then struck again, and bounded again,
and struck again, till, crumpled and broken and no
longer recognizable, it came to rest on a sandy bay beside
the river. A tiara of flames, pale in the daylight, rose
through black smoke near Phantom Ranch. The body of
the pilot lay apart, arms outstretched in the attidude of
crucifixion. There was no sign of injury, only the eyes
were closed and the grace of youth was lapped in sleep.

It was Louis.

In this strange place no one seemed distressed; they
stood gravely looking on while Louis' young wife went
forward and knelt by the body, slipping her arm beneath
the shoulders and lifting him into a sitting position
propped against her thigh. He was limp, his head rolled
sideways, she stroked the hair back from his temples.

They made such a tender group that the blind man
murmured "*Pietà*," as he watched them.

"Listen how she whispers to him," said the deaf man.

The others could scarcely catch the whisper, but the
deaf man caught it.

The Indian boy came up and looked on. "He all

right, missy," he said; "he all right soon." Jacqueline
looked up with an expression of such radiance that they
all felt themselves to be in the presence of some miraculous
transfiguration. "He's all right *now*," she said, "look, he
opens his eyes," and again she bent down to whisper, while
the figure stirred slightly in her arms. He stirred as he
might have stirred in their bed, slenderly waking at dawn
and turning voluptuously towards her with whom he
had shared the early passion of the darkened hours. Her
finger-tips ran over his brows in the tenderness of a
caress which held all the delicacy of tired-out physical
love and all the closeness of other kinds of love as well.
The gesture of her fingers running over his hair expressed
the painful tenderness that one may feel for the physical
body of another person, but the radiance of her face
expressed the spiritual closeness between them, when
they could imagine that neither life nor death nor sex
had anything to do with their bond.

It was pleasant to watch him coming gradually to life
again after his temporary death, and pleasant above all
to reflect that the anguish of anxiety she had endured in
her mortal days was now resolved into its solution. She
had lived, seeing him fly away towards danger, pain, and
destruction; for days she had known nothing of his fate;
and she herself, hovering between her living and her
dying (for the transition had not been so very rapid as
they marched from the Rim down into the canyon and
it had taken them all several days to adjust themselves to
the new arrangement), she herself had undergone all
mortal anxieties for the fate of the loved body. She had
known the suffering that that uncertainty can bring. Are
the bones protruding from limbs that once I loved? Is
that dear head smashed in? *Tam cari capitis*, the poet said;
that dear, dear head; that darling head; that anguish of
protective love aroused by the threat of damage; those
curls matted with the blood and brains that I have never

seen? Nurses in hospitals (she had thought to herself during those days) are accustomed to those sights; they take them for granted; their point of view is the practical point of view; a broken limb is a thing to be mended, jointed together again as a carpenter splices two jaggy bits of wood; a fractured skull may be a more delicate operation; mending and grafting a shattered face may be an even more delicate operation; but how little these nurses and carving surgeons know of what goes on in the minds of the poor ignorant unprofessional people, stuck down in the waiting-room, waiting for news, getting very sparse information, being soothed by a professional voice they do not believe in although they would like to believe.

Jacqueline had been thinking all these things to herself, in the muddled turmoil that the brain gets into under exceptional stress.

Now here was Louis, dead yet alive. He moved gently in her arms. "Louis," she said, "my love, my darling."

"Jacqueline," he said, recognizing her as his eyes opened.

"You are not hurt?" she asked.

"I am all right," he replied.

§

He got up gradually on to his feet. He stood upright again and stood, a tall young man looking with surprise at Phantom Ranch and his young wife.

"Jacqueline?" he said, puzzled.

"Louis," she replied, confident.

There seemed nothing left for the other people but to go away. They drifted off, leaving Louis and Jacqueline to each other. There is nothing else to do when love comes in and excludes everyone else as unnecessary and a hindrance. They were able to observe the pair from a

distance, wandering vaguely among the rocks. It seemed
that they played like children, devising little games and
bumping their heads together as they stooped too eagerly
over their inventions. The others were constantly coming
on their traces. They had had water and stones and
flowers to play with. Here they had built a miniature
castle of sand buttressed by coloured fragments and had
scooped a complicated system of moats and canals around
it, with little dams and lakes and bridges,—Louis seemed
still to remember that he had once been an engineer
—and tiny roads beautifully paved with shards leading
away as though in a whisper towards the immensities of
the canyons. In another place they had left a wreath,
made of flowers the others could not find growing anywhere; they had jettisoned it on their way. In yet another
place they had left a water-mill, its green sails cut from
the leaves of a yucca; they had set it to be turned by a
minute waterfall and it flung rainbow drops in spray,
imitating in miniature the wide rainbows that straddled
the rocks. A gentle poetry about all their movements
redeemed them from a silly childishness; a simplicity of
grace and love hung round their complete unselfcon-
sciousness. At night they never came with the others into
the ranch huts, but slept somewhere in the open, and then
it was possible, nay, inevitable to imagine without
impertinence their young limbs interlaced and the breath
delicately ruffling the soft hair. Mr. Dale, who was too
much touched to be caustic, called them Paolo and
Francesca. "They don't need to recall the happiness of
times past," he said, "for those times are with them for
ever."

§

Louis was however still sufficiently attached to the
outside world to be able to give his companions some

account of it. His degree of attachment seemed slight, no stronger than a few threads ready to snap if he chose to float away, but at moments he seemed quite willing and even eager to talk. He had always been a very masculine young man, and neither the passionate love which he had enjoyed before nor the idealized love he was enjoying now could entirely absorb him. Jacqueline sat patient while he talked. She was not interested in what he was saying, but she was prepared to wait for the moment when she could get him back to herself if in the meantime she might listen to the tones of his voice without paying attention to his words and could let her eyes rove over the appreciative expressions of his hearers. She thought that they admired him, and that sufficed her. It was fitting that they should do so.

The wireless had kept them informed of the major events, but there were details which Louis was able to fill in. He began by speaking dispassionately but with sorrow. It appeared that the lessons of the last war had been unavailing and that the American leaders with incredible trustfulness had once more been taken by surprise. "Of course this time they had but little choice," he exclaimed, while Jacqueline thought how beautiful he looked when he frowned, "after the treaties imposed by *force majeure*. For what else was it but *force majeure*, my friends? It was all very well for this great nation to declare that in the interests of humanity peace must be restored to the earth, but the fact was that after the total subjugation of Europe and Great Britain the United States were reluctant to go on fighting alone. An alliance with the greatest power the world had ever seen appeared to be the safer policy. The offer that Germany put forward then had all the semblance of expediency and reason. Mutual destruction is absurd, they said; absurd and unnecessary; co-operation is the only hope, humanly and economically; let us co-operate now, and save what is left in order to re-build. Leave us the Old World and we will leave you the New, or at any rate a good part of it. You shall have all your own continent to yourselves, North America, that is, including Canada which we could easily retain but which in our generosity and desire for a fair understanding we will allot to you; the republics of Latin America of course must decide for themselves. You, my friends, will remember these pronouncements as though they had been uttered this morning. You will remember also the conflict of argument that they provoked. A crueller test had never been applied to human judgement. We know now that human judgement decided wrong, and some of us may be proud to recall that we protested at the time. Our protests were vain, and the agreement so ironically known to us as the Pacific Charter was duly ratified in Berlin. Our leaders still believed in the pledging of a word that no schoolboy would have credited."

He spoke quietly but deeply. It was manifest that he had both thought and felt. He had suffered, but he had not been content to suffer blindly; he had also examined the causes of his suffering for himself.

"After all that had happened!" he said. "After all the betrayals, the broken assurances, the secret scheming! Is it impossible for humanity to learn? Or is it impossible for us to connect any given event with its predecessors and probable successors? to observe any given event, not as an isolated adventure, but as a drop in the stream of causality? It seems so. We cannot learn. Experience means nothing. Oh," he passionately said, "how foolish, foolish, and foolish again we are! How impossible to express the foolishness and wrongness of this human race, how impossible to express their striving after their highest aspirations and their fall down into the lowest trough. Poor us! poor fallible us! How pitiable we are! Whenever we feel tempted to judge and condemn one another, we should return to the realization of our pitifulness, which seems to be the beginning and end of all judgement."

Mr. Dale glanced at Mrs. Temple. He remembered that she had scolded him for being scornful and intolerant. Her words had bitten him deeply enough for him to remember them. He was not accustomed to being scolded since he had no friends intimate enough to criticize him; yet Mrs. Temple, who was only an acquaintance not a friend, had taken it upon herself to reprove him in her gentle way.

He glanced across at her, but she was not looking in his direction. She was sitting propped against a boulder, her hands clasped round her knees. She scarcely seemed to be listening to Louis, but to be following some train of thought of her own. He supposed that she had heard and read remarks such as Louis' too often, for, after all, in spite of Jacqueline's admiration, he was really saying no more than any moderately intelligent young man had said some millions of times since 1939.

Yet for all her abstraction he noticed that she preserved the peculiar quality of awareness which was hers. She was always there, although she might seem to be "not there." Queer woman, he thought; and discovered in himself a desire to know her better. In their present circumstances it seemed likely that he would have every opportunity for doing so.

Louis looked round, fearing that he had talked too much, but seeing that he held his audience he went on.

"We are an adequately representative collection here," he said, "American, English, Polish, Czech, French. . . . We all lived through that strange time with its fears and confusions and hatreds. Some of us saw our countries blasted, some of us kept our lives and nothing else. There were moments when we were threatened with a suspension of all rational standards and turned into an animal snapping in defence, grabbing at its food. The rational being should never be reduced to such a state. It is a vilification that humanity should never be asked to undergo; a grotesque distortion, a twisting of the heroic qualities. That those qualities should still have shown themselves remains to our credit I suppose, if we must insist on looking round for one good thing to say of war. But if we felt hatred also and the desire for revenge, shall that be blamed upon us? Hatred that loathly passion! With a remnant of shame we tried to call it justifiable moral indignation. But to be truthful not hypocritical let's admit that in the confusion few of us could spare time to estimate war itself through the soul. The material bewilderment was too great for that. The physical and emotional turbulence were too urgently in the foreground. Our bodies, our hearts, our needs, in what order were we to arrange them? We had no leisure to survey the dreadful landscape we had created for ourselves; we lived for the moment, since the future held no probability. We had begun recently to believe that the world was in process of readjustment,—I do not say that it was an adjustment to our liking, but at least the planet seemed to be steadying itself on its axis,—and now with another push it rocks again and we ourselves return to the brink of madness."

Mrs. Temple gently intervened.

"You promised, M. Louis, to tell us something of what you had been able to observe."

"Forgive me, I got carried away. My wife will tell you that it is my bad habit. What I myself have been able to observe? So little! You see, I became a unit once more, no longer an independent creature. Mentally I returned to the dullness of being a machine waiting to receive orders; physically I returned to the sharpness of being a machine trained to execute them. That is an exhilaration! Nerve, skill, decision, all at their finest pitch,—the *bravura* of the air . . . but I get carried away again. You ask for facts. Alas, I had so short a while, not a week. The big items of the news you know from the radio, you know as much as I. Rumour says that the air-borne troop landings are far greater and more continuous than the radio admits; it cannot conceal their occurrence but it is not allowed to reveal their magnitude. It seems, in fact, that swarms of ants are crawling over the prairies; I have flown some way on reconnaissance and I have seen for myself. America puts a big boot down on one cluster of them, but next hour there are more, always more. Destroying them is like throwing pebbles into the sea in the hope that the beach will disappear."

"But what can they hope to accomplish?"

"Madame, how often did we say that in the last war: what can they hope to accomplish?"

No one answered his question.

"There have been some fine battles, though," he said, looking very young and excitable again. He turned towards Loraine. "These countrymen of yours, Miss Driscoll, these American flyers, my, they know their job! We always used to talk of the New World; well, if taking to the air was a symptom of a new world, those boys live up to it: they must have been born with wings. Their mothers pushed them over the edge of a nest instead of sending them off in nice warm underwear on their walk to school. The swooping fights I've seen! Your country was planned for such things. Your plains now crawl with armies while your squadrons wheel above them. That is how it should be. Forgive me for saying so, I do not forget that it is your country which is now at war; but you see although with my soul I hate war, with my body I am a fighting man, and when I see such a battlefield and such forces so magnificently set I must respond with my blood. It leaps, it applauds. I forget that I should think it terrible, and see only that it is superb."

"Aren't you rather lapsing into the confusion of thought you spoke of just now?" said Mr. Dale mildly.

"Sir, I am. But if you had seen what I have seen you would share the confusion with me. Not for long, perhaps, but in the momentary recollection. Everything was on so grand a scale, the sky and the earth so empty until they filled with those murderous men, and then there were hordes above and hordes below, and it was difficult to know which were the angels of light and which were the angels of darkness flying in the heavens, but it was easy enough to know that the masses creeping on the ground were the imps of an evil to be destroyed."

Mr. Dale looked dubious but refrained from argument.

"I saw your brother, Miss Driscoll," said Louis turning again to Loraine. "You remember how he used to pretend that it bored him to become a qualified pilot? He used to say he did it only in order to please your father; he told me his allowance would be cut down if he didn't agree. *Quel blagueur!* I never believed him. His nerve was in the Air really all the time; he wasn't much interested in anything else and that was why he could pretend so successfully to be interested in nothing at all. Well, he was splendid. You've seen him in his flying helmet, looking like a god about to soar into his natural element. That's how he looked every time before he went into battle, only then there was something in his face which you have never seen there. You have seen him only when he was going off on an ordinary flight, never when he was going to kill or be killed. He couldn't help being beautiful; he couldn't alter the sculpture of his features, and he was quite well aware of their advantages, but he was unaware of the change that came over him whenever orders arrived. He ceased to be Hollywood's ideal then and became something real. To watch him standing beside his plane was like hearing music. It was beautiful and alarming. No one dared speak to him except the mechanics and the groundsmen. He looked like a saint inviting death. And he didn't know it; for the first time in his life he wasn't thinking of his looks or of their effect on other people. Then he would take off and be gone for as many hours as his fuel would last him, and when he returned the control-room would get only the barest report from him. So many of the enemy shot down, so many damaged; but never any extra account of how he had done it. He always flew a single-seater plane, so nobody could check up exactly on what he had done. I think he was a lone bird by nature. They offered him a double-plane with a gunner, but he wouldn't have it. He liked to be on his own. Perhaps you knew that, Miss Driscoll?"

"I certainly knew he didn't care much for anything but himself and what he wanted and what he foresaw."

The others thought that this remark was made with normal sisterly acerbity. Mrs. Temple alone saw that Loraine was so agitated that she had hardly brought herself to answer. She was just about to dash in and help the girl when Louis himself went on gravely.

"You cheapen him, Miss Driscoll. You say that he cared for nothing but himself and what he wanted. That's true. I daresay your parents suffered from his egotism in their home. I daresay you suffered from it yourself. You saw his egotism only in the sense that it was a nuisance and an inconvenience and an exasperation. The spoilt son, the privileged brother, and all those things which mean much to you Driscolls, inside the family circle. To the women to whom he made a pretence of love he appears as a different character; he appears as the charmer, the gay, the rich, the dashing young man; they don't care what he is like at home so long as he makes love skilfully and gives them a good time all round. But to us who saw him on the North or the South Rim,—on the edge of life or of death,—he seemed different again. I don't know which you will think was the true Robert Driscoll; I daresay he couldn't have told us himself."

L

No one seemed to notice that he had dropped into the past tense. Mrs. Temple was sure Loraine had not noticed although her agitation was still to be read in her twisting fingers and bitten lip. This evident emotion on the part of a sister seemed excessive, but then there had always been some riddle about Loraine which the older woman had never resolved.

§

The next time she came upon Louis and Jacqueline alone she asked him outright. The two were sitting by themselves near the river, playing one of their innocent games. They looked so young and carefree that Mrs. Temple hesitated to interrupt them with what might be the introduction of tragedy, but then she reflected that tragedy in the human sense of the word had no existence in this place. She approached them, they looked up with their friendly smiles.

"M. Louis," she said, coming straight to the point, "I wanted to ask you, has Robert Driscoll been killed?"

"He was killed on the third day, Mrs. Temple, out over the Painted Desert."

"Why didn't you tell his sister yesterday when you were talking to her about him?"

"Well, you see, I wasn't sure how she would take it. I haven't been here long enough to know. I consulted Jacqueline and she wasn't sure either. So I thought I would begin by preparing her mind."

"That was very considerate of you. You seem to be a young man of some imagination."

"Are you ironical or serious, Mrs. Temple? It is all rather confusing and one's values are disturbed. Or perhaps I should say that one's values are coming right for the first time and that it is the readjustment which is puzzling. Anyway, we could not decide. Then we thought of asking you to tell her."

"Why me? Why not Miss Carlisle, who is in charge of Loraine and all those young girls?"

Louis and Jacqueline both went off into peals of the gayest French laughter.

"The good Miss Carlisle? That poor worried English stick, who for all the years she has spent in America has never mentally moved a mile away from the playing-fields of a girls' school? No, dear Mrs. Temple. Miss Carlisle just succeeded in getting her charges punctually in to dinner at the hotel,—did you ever know that Royer terrorized her?—but beyond these few scraps of discipline she had with them a contact less intimate than a shepherd has with his sheep. How much do you think she has ever known of those high-spirited rebellious girls? No, no. It is for you, and not for Miss Carlisle, to tell Loraine that the bones of her brother will bleach upon the Painted Desert."

"Thank you very much," said Mrs. Temple; "but if you exact this not agreeable task of me you must tell me the manner of Robert Driscoll's death. His sister will ask. I must warn you that I did not take to Robert Driscoll; he did not take my fancy in the least. Yet from the way you spoke of him yesterday I think you saw something in him which I overlooked. I should have guessed it; I blame myself for judging too superficially. It is a mistake I have not yet learned to correct."

"He was inspired," said Louis. "Men have two natures, and one of them they keep concealed. It may be either the finer or the baser nature; in Robert's case it was the finer. I did not like to say in the hearing of all those people yesterday and especially not in the hearing of that young girl his sister, but what I thought in my own mind was that anyone seeing him stand beside his plane ready in

his flying helmet would have understood the meaning of
the classic *pédérastie héroïque*. He was young, he was
dedicated, he was to be worshipped. The very shape of
his plane made a wholeness with him: together they were
the winged victory, the *Nike apteros*."

"In modern terms."

"In modern terms. And what added a significance of
modernity to it, Mrs. Temple, was the invisible speed of
the propellor-blades once they had started to revolve.
It was like a curious development of sculpture, again in
modern terms; almost a new form of art. The character
of sculpture is that it should be static, is it not? that it
should be at rest; that it should catch and immobilize an
attitude, a gesture. The seized moment is complete in
itself; there can be no necessity or possibility of change
consequent upon it. The most that sculpture has hitherto
attempted to do is to suggest movement, and it might be
argued that even the suggestion of movement is 'impure'
in the sculptor's art, since it is contrary to the static
principle. Thus, if you wished to split hairs of argument,
you might contend that the Victory of Samothrace was
an 'impure' example of the sculptor's art, since she
seemed ready to fly off her stand at the top of the stairs
in the Louvre, but that the Charioteer of Delphi was
'pure' in his rigidity. He could not move, although he
might be carried along in his chariot. Now Robert
Driscoll, seated in his cockpit, was as austere and as
motionless, though far more beautiful. The wings of his
plane, stretched out in their eternal span, were motionless too; and only the propeller-blades revolving so fast
that they appeared as a solid disc to the eye, supplied the
velocity to this composition which so oddly combined
the static and the active."

"So this young man," said Mrs. Temple, "whom we
all set down as a rotter and a cad . . ."

"Was possibly both. But he was a brave man too. I

think he knew he would not last long. I saw him that
last day; he was flying alone, separated from his squadron,
I think he had separated himself on purpose, and I saw
him fly straight at a shoal of enemy planes, bombers with
their fighter escort. What lunatic is this? I asked myself,
for no single fighter could have lived in the heart of that
wasps' nest. But he went in amongst them, and never in
my life have I seen such a display of virtuosity crammed
into five minutes. He was very fast; faster than any of
their machines, I should say; and he dived and swooped
and soared and came down on them again, till they must
have blinked their eyes trying to follow which way he
had gone. I blinked myself, for he was between me and
the sun, flashing like a silver fish as the sun twisted on his
wings. They got him, of course, but not before he had
shot six of them in flames to the ground, and then his
own turn came and he went down headlong and his
plane lay still. I went back later in the day and landed
close beside the wreck to have a look. There was nobody
about at the time either in the sky or on the ground; it
was right out in a very lonely part of the desert; there
was nothing but this smashed-up thing and the six other
things scattered all round him as though he had arranged
them there to humiliate them into doing him honour.
It was awfully silent out there. I had meant to bring back
his body if there was anything left of it."

He stopped.

"Go on," said Mrs. Temple. "Tell me everything."

"You will not tell his sister this part," said Louis. "It
is better that she should think of him beautiful as she
knew him. He was burnt, Mrs. Temple. I do not know
if you have ever seen a man who has been burnt like that.
It is unrecognizable, and this thing like a charred black
log lay out on the colours of the Painted Desert. I rolled
big stones up to his body, and covered the pile over with
a slab of rock flat as a table, so that no animal or scavenger

bird should touch him. It was the best I could do before
I flew away and left him there."

"You did not bring his wrist-watch or anything that
I could give his sister?"

"Mrs. Temple, I perceive that indeed you have never
seen a man burnt like that. His wrist-watch? There was
no wrist to bring it from."

§

She wondered how she had best set about the task of
informing Loraine, and wished rather ruefully that
people throughout her life had not always assumed that
her shoulders were strong enough to carry anything.
Here was Louis, never dreaming of sparing her the full
cruelty of his picture. Of course he could not know that
her own son had been lost flying, and that the words
had stirred up all the anguish of speculation over the
unknown details of his fate. She could not blame Louis,
but she did wish sometimes that people would remember
that she also was a human being with possible troubles of
her own, instead of accepting her as an automaton for
helping them with theirs. She wondered why it was. She
always kept very quietly to her own corner, never seeking
people out or inviting their confidences, yet they always
ended by coming her way.

She was glad now to be alone, sitting on a boulder in
that place of flowers and spray. The canyon was not
forbidding here; the river was wide and the light streamed
down unimpeded; the red cliffs rose in their enchanted
architecture, in such variety that the gaze could wander
over them all day without exhausting their noble fanci-
fulness. She could never cease to marvel at the fabulous
place, which seemed to have been conceived and created
in one gigantic effort of an unimaginable imagination,
rather than carved grain by grain in the natural process

of aeons. It was easier to believe in the spontaneous freak of a deity, than in the slow sequence of coincidences which had at length produced this unity.

Helen Temple was one of those people to whom the silence or the sounds of nature come as a relief after the human voice. There were times when the human voice made her want to put her hands over her ears, and during the whole of her adult life it had been her practice to escape for several hours each day. Sometimes it had been into the inhospitability of her bedroom; of late, it had been into the enormous silence of the Painted Desert; now it was into the no less enormous concert-hall of the canyon that she made her way alone. She had never decided whether the orchestration of the canyon was thunderous or subdued. Sometimes it seemed her ear was filled as though she held a sea-shell against it; sometimes the whisper of the finest flute came through, the note of a bird, the chirrup of a little animal or insect, the spirtle from a spring, the drip of water from an overhanging rock on to a stone beneath. Through the strong continuous roar of the river, to which one became accustomed as to the roar of traffic, the treble of these minute sounds became more acute, more precious. Delicacy contrasted with power. Which did she prefer? When one considered this question the world split itself into halves like cutting an apple. Was it impossible ever to keep the apple whole? a globe to hold entire in the hand?

Yet at the same time it seemed to her living at the bottom of the canyon that all things mixed and mingled themselves into a rounded globe such as she had always desired to find. Thus all the senses came into play, and she found herself less and less able to distinguish between sound and sight, the aural and the visual; and even the sense of touch became confused, so that as she ran her fingers down the leaf of an aloe pricking herself deliberately on a spike the slight pain of the prick made her remember some note of music, some line of poetry, some physical or mental pain she had once endured, and mixed itself also with the steep grandeurs of the canyon and the flat coloured emptinesses of the Painted Desert, and the little bright drop of blood on her finger-tip had also its significance.

She remembered Louis' words about sculpture, "almost a new form of art," and now sitting alone she understood fully what he had meant: that everything was really one thing, if only we had the sense to apprehend it. It seemed a deep truth, simply expressed. It comprised all the different facets of truth, scientific, philosophical, religious, astronomical, human. They all must meet at some perspective point, but until one could reach that perspective point of meeting, confusion must continue within the concept of the limited human mind.

We are all, she thought, at the stage of the early draughtsmen who had not discovered the simple secret of the vanishing-point and who thereby were compelled to represent every thing as on almost the same plane. They had some sort of idea that one object came behind or in front of another object but could not express the idea on a two-dimensional surface. Once discovered, the secret seemed simple even to a child.

She was humble enough to suppose that the same might apply to many other apparent mysteries.

In her past life she had made an effort to read books about relativity. It had been a pleasurable effort, since she never undertook such studies unless she wanted to; she was not the sort of woman to undertake them just because they happened to be fashionable. On the contrary, she had felt humble and ashamed at even attempting to understand such things so far beyond the power of her own thought; she would never have boasted in public about her tiny corner of conquered knowledge; she would have receded, rather, into a pretence of ignorance.

She knew well that she was incapable of grasping the enormous truths that she was trying with her tiny brain to surround.

When she read these books about relativity an occasional streak of comprehension had crossed her mind. She had thought she just began to understand; she had tried to catch the flash of understanding as it lit her dark sky; then it was gone, burning her as it passed, but leaving nothing behind: an instant of illumination, a rocket soaring into the black sky, smashing itself high up into a few ephemeral falling stars; no more. They fell not to earth, one knew not where; they went out, extinguished in the empyrean; only the stick fell to earth, dead, exhausted; the rocket-stick that came down somewhere on the ground long after the idea, the ideology, had gone up into the heavens to fail, to fall, because the ideology of man was insufficient in its support.

It was pleasant to be able to sit alone and think vaguely about such things with no responsibility attached. There was a pleasure and a luxury in such solitude; a sense of having indeterminate hours ahead, with no engagements, no appointments, no obligations, no likelihood of any impingement from the exterior world. The planes passed overhead from time to time, but they were impersonal; they went on their swift way leaving her to her reposeful way a mile within the earth, and even the planes in this new comprehension that seemed to be dawning over her mixed not incompatibly with her thoughts and with the canyon in its sights and sounds.

§

"Helen."

She looked round. There was Mr. Dale, and she had the impression that he had been watching her for some time. She was not pleased. Moreover she was surprised by his use of her Christian name. He had always been most correct in his mode of address and she had liked him for not taking advantage of the prevalent fashion.

She must have looked at him coldly, for he moved a few paces away as though aware of his double trespass.

"I fear I interrupt you, Mrs. Temple."

"You startled me, I admit. I thought I was alone. The river makes so much sound that anyone can approach without his footsteps being audible."

"So I disturb you?"

"You did, but it doesn't matter."

"What a truthful person you appear to be," he said comfortably. "You make no bones about admitting that I disturbed your meditations, but since you add that it now doesn't matter, I feel that I may take you at your word, having done the damage for which you so rightly reprove me, and may continue to impose my company upon you for a while. I observe that you have recently been enjoying a company more romantic than mine, that of Paul and Virginia," and he pointed to the interlaced monogram of L and J which Louis and Jacqueline had left drawn in flower-petals on the strand.

"Paul and Virginia,—they were Paolo and Francesca last time you mentioned them."

"Well, they are pretty creatures, by whatever name they go. I sometimes think him rather a sententious young prig, but then I am immediately disarmed by his sincerity and by her pathetic admiration. He suffers from the fault of the generous young, which is to indulge too much in generalizations."

"I do not think you would have found him sententious had you heard him talking just now. He was telling me about the death of Robert Driscoll."

"What, has he been scuppered, that ineffable . . ."

"Hush. I know. But you must not say it. Yes, he was

shot down, and Louis has charged me with the task of telling his sister."

"You will not enjoy doing that. I remember you always had a peculiar feeling about that attractive but very ordinary girl. You seemed to think she was marked out for tragedy in some undefined way. Perhaps the brother's death was the explanation."

"Oh no, I do not believe that. It was something much more personal, much more unusual. Moreover I have an idea that the tragedy, whatever it was, has already taken place, although I have noticed a change in Loraine lately, since we have been down here. I mean: a change in her expression, a sort of liberation, as though the thing (whatever it was) no longer mattered."

"Rape, probably," said Mr. Dale rudely. "That would have been personal enough, though not so very unusual. She is a pretty girl, pretty in a sleek subtle way like a line-drawing on vellum, and damned into the bargain by an elusive purity which is the most dangerous form of sex-appeal and makes the brutal male want to capture and conquer. You must not romanticize these things too much, Mrs. Temple. They are, believe me, entirely a matter of the way the flesh is arranged over the bone; they bear no relation to the soul within."

"When you speak like that you tempt me to believe that your own experience has been bad. Unfortunate, I mean; not wicked. Bad and sad.—Please don't imagine that I am trying to discover anything about your private life in the past. I know nothing of it, and I don't want to know."

"Oh, shy pigeon!" he said, laughing with a heartier amusement than he usually betrayed. I "didn't suspect you of trying to pry. I didn't suspect you of trying to play the role of the sympathetic woman meeting the lonely man. I am readily bored by women, Helen. I have never had any intimate friend in my life, but on the whole I have preferred the companionship of men to the cloying, prying self-sacrificing love of women. Not that any woman ever loved me. I am too unattractive for that. Nature did not arrange my flesh over my bones in the right way, a serious omission on the part of Nature which I rather resent since I flatter myself that I might have proved quite a skilful lover and an admirable father, proud of my sons, interested in my daughters, companionable to my wife. But that was not to be my fate. Do I bore you?"

"I think I have heard that question from you several times before now, and I have always truthfully replied 'No'."

"All right then, I will go on. You are honest enough to send me packing when you want to. It has never been my habit to talk about myself or even to think much about myself. An uninteresting subject. I am a selfish man, I suppose, if it is selfish to want your existence to yourself and never to allow it to be disturbed by anyone else. I made up my mind to this singleness on my twenty-second birthday. My father, may his spirit rest in peace, gave a coming-of-age party for me and as I passed along the restaurant corridor I caught sight of myself in a full-length mirror and saw how irremediably plain, plump and pasty I already was. I cut my wisdom teeth with a rush that night. Suet-face, pudding-face, I said to my reflection, the love of women is not for you. It was an unkind moment, which I celebrated by putting out my tongue at my own image in the crude rude gesture of the street-urchin. Churlish, captious character, I said, going on to address the inner not the outer man, the friendship of men is not for you either."

He paused, waiting to see whether she would make the obvious comforting comment that most women would have made. To his relief she did not. She only said "What you have just been telling me explains why you were so waspish about the good looks and sexual charm of the boys and girls up at the hotel."

"Suppressed envy. Yes, of course. Thank you for clarifying something I had never analysed for myself. Anyway, I determined from that evening of my birthday-party to live my life, keeping my speculations purely objective. The bundle of flesh known as Lester Dale was to have no existence beyond the label of a name tied on to it. I never desired a friend nor had one, disliking intimacy and disliking obligations even more. Independence was what I wanted and what I got. I've known other men of course; travelled with them even, sat by camp fires with them at night, but they were always men on whom I could depend for silence. At the end of six weeks or six months we could part with a nod and a 'well, good luck to you,' nothing more. All that had mattered was that we could both keep our tempers when the tent blew away."

He glared at her as though expecting to be challenged.

"As for women," he went on, "I took myself off whenever they threatened to interfere with me. If a woman began to attract me, even if the poor soul remained quite unaware of it, it constituted interference. It was all part of my settled policy.—You smile?"

"Only because I cannot help finding you most entertaining, Mr. Dale. Are you sure that your settled policy shouldn't rather be called pride? One of the seven deadly sins, you know."

"Pride is a Janus," he said, "whose other head is called humility. Remember that before you condemn me; not that you ever condemn.—As a matter of fact, it wasn't entirely pride. There was a good pinch of common sense mixed in with it. I had noticed early in life that men had their values and that women had theirs, but that generally speaking those values were so different that the only

common meeting-ground was either in the dance-hall or
the bed. From both those rallying-points I felt myself
to be by nature debarred. So, guided by a gleam of
self-protective sagacity, I kept away. Do you blame
me?"

"Of course I don't blame you, but did you never regret
your settled policy?"

His comically round face suddenly looked sad. She had
always thought of his face as a hollowed turnip into
which a child had stuck candles for eyes. Now something
had blown out the candles and the little flame of mischief
had gone.

"Did I regret? You must know as well as I do that to
any person of too intense a sensibility life is one long
process of switching over from one mood to another.
Traffic lights!" he said, regaining his sense of fun. "They
switch from red to green along one's street and one ought
to be thankful if one can arrange for the warning transition of the amber."

"But if you gave up so much," said Mrs. Temple, who
knew better than to be taken in by his jokes and meant
to press him down on to the point now that he had
perched himself there, "if you gave up so much, what did
you really esteem in the old life? Not riches, not luxury,
not self-indulgence, not comfort even; not material
comfort or the very ordinary demands of mankind, human
affection, home, roots, ties. . . . Public affairs do not seem
to have claimed you either. What then?"

"I floated," he said; "floated. In a warm private sea
of useless out-of-date ideas. In theory I thought myself
a liberal. In practice I did nothing to encourage the ideas
in which I believed. I think I knew them to be so dead
that no little breath of mine could blow them back into
a flame. They were as remote from modern life as the
eighteenth century in which I should have liked to live.
Violence and competition were distasteful to me. The

furniture of my mind, though I never owned a house to match it, was Sheraton and egg-shell china, with a grandfather clock ticking in the corner."

"Courtesy, gentleness and the humanities," said Mrs. Temple. "Burgundy rather than beer; conversation rather than the telephone."

"It sounds very mild, does it not? But please do not think that I was egotistically indifferent to the lot of unfortunate mortals. It worried me very much indeed to reflect that all men were not equally situated; that owing to our social system equality of opportunity was denied; that the most deserving were not necessarily the most prosperous. The gifts dispensed by Nature we could not control; we could no more alter the child's mental outfit than we could remodel his physical; we could bestow neither aptitude nor beauty. But there were other things we could have adjusted, and I assure you that it distressed me considerably to observe how very little we were doing to adjust them."

"Yet you yourself didn't take any practical steps. . . ."

"Ah, you put your finger on my weakness. I dare say you will set it down to pride again, though personally I prefer to set it down to humility: I felt I could do so little that it wasn't worth doing at all. How readily one makes excuses for one's own failures. So I contented myself with theorizing, I dare say because it suited my disdainful nature better. Have you ever observed the habits of the marmot?"

"Please inform me."

"Well, the marmot is a paunchy little animal who digs himself a hole and stuffs the entrance with a wad of chewed grass, congealed by his own saliva. He stays inside, secure from enemies and winter weather. In summer days he comes out and suns himself on the pleasant slopes. That was me. My theories took the place of the saliva."

"The war must have fitted very badly into your scheme of things."

"Very badly indeed. I cannot tell you how comical I looked in battle-dress. My company sergeant-major was a professional caricaturist of genius and I think I may say that he found me invaluable as a model."

"So you went into the army, did you?" said Mrs. Temple, scrutinizing him closely. "I should have expected a man of your . . . enlightenment to be a pacifist."

"Oh, I was, I was. I still am. But there seemed no alternative then between running away from the damned thing and helping to stop it. You see, unlike some people, I had no justification for persuading myself that I could be of more value in another sphere—or another hemisphere. I wished I had. Some people seem to enjoy war, or some aspects of it. I daresay that playboy Robert Driscoll did, but personally I was aware of nothing but a great distaste. Also I was frightened. Oh yes, I assure you. I suppose I was born into the sort of timidity that suffers from apprehensions. I always felt that I could bear any certainty however unpleasant; that if one knew a disaster was scheduled to overtake one at a specified time one would be prepared for it; but that the supreme uncertainty of war was the last thing I ought to be called upon to bear. So you see how gladly I should have welcomed a conviction of my own importance, a persuasion that I should be advancing the cause of civilization much better by removing myself as far from the scene of peril as possible."

"The sensations of fear were so erratic, weren't they?" said Mrs. Temple. "Sometimes one felt completely indifferent, or even rather interested to see what was going to happen next; then an uncontrollable dread would shake one physically and morally. . . . But what I minded most, and most consistently, was the inability to grasp the total picture. The thing was too enormous, both in its events and its implications; one's brain seemed the size of a bullet. One felt that there ought to be some comprehensive formula somewhere if only it wouldn't elude one; some formula which would embrace such mighty passions, such convulsions of order, such miniatures of heroism, such hatred and such devotion. . . . I express myself in platitudes, but the exasperation of my insufficiency was a red-hot iron in my soul, a very real thing and no phrase."

"You come nearer now," he said very gravely, "to the centre which is related to your bewilderment in those days,—the appalling sorrow one experienced, the grief which I compare in all reverence to the grief of Mary contemplating the dying Christ upon the cross; a sorrow not human, not personal, though it embraced all humanity, an anguish I cannot speak of, even to you."

She was so much surprised by the change in his tone that she scarcely noticed the "even" which had slipped into his last three words.

"So that was how you felt about the war, was it?"

For the first time, she saw agony come over the careful mask of his face. His voice, usually pleasant, tore like ripped calico.

"All that, Helen, and more. It was the torture, at first, of not knowing where right lay, or wrong; the torture, next, of seeing that wrong could only be controlled by another wrong, by an imitation of the same folly; the seismic overthrow of principles and ethics; the condoning, through imitation, of the argument of force. Seeing ourselves compelled to behave in such and such a fashion because other men chose to set the example of that fashion. . . . I have wondered, since, in bad hours, whether the path we chose was the right path, the best one. It seemed plain enough at the time, whilst we were in the middle of it, but now . . ."

"Oh, never doubt!" she said. "That is perhaps the

M

bitterest aftermath of all, to allow such a question to creep in. It is not to be admitted. There was no question of choosing our path; we had no choice. We hated fighting but we had to fight. In order to overcome a thing we hated even worse."

"That is your sincere conviction?" he said, staring at her.

"It is perhaps the most sincere conviction I hold. I think you hold it also?"

"Yes," he said, "I hold it also. We did right. We had no choice. Standing away from it now, at a distance, I see what we were unable to see at the time, and what the people up there above the Rim are no doubt unable to see now whilst they are in the midst of it. I see that it never matters who the enemy is. We became so hypnotized by the spectral words Nazi and Führer that we forgot the real enemy is always Evil and Folly. The Führer might be a symbol; but he was not a comprehensive symbol. Evil is greater even than he. Hitler must acknowledge that one suzerain. Unlike Christ who, taken also as a symbol, need not acknowledge love's perfection as greater than himself, for they are co-equal. It was darkness that we were fighting; darkness which is eternal, and which depends for its existence on no one man, nor for its annihilation upon his overthrow."

§

They saw the deaf man coming along towards them. Ever since the day when he had thrown his ear-trumpet down on a rock and had stood listening with incredulous delight to its clatter, he had walked about with a pocket wireless-set as though he could not be parted from the world of sound. He laid it down now beside them, a neat little case no bigger than a kodak.

"News," he said. He stood gazing down at it as though the fact that it could talk and that he could hear was far more remarkable than what it was about to say.

"Listeners have already heard that an important battle has been joined between enemy forces and the forces of the United States in the Californian desert. Some further details have just come to hand though the confusion is necessarily considerable. It would appear that some thousands of war-planes arrived over the city of San Francisco at an early hour this morning and were immediately engaged in combat by our fighters, but that owing to their superiority in numbers and speed a proportion of them were able to pass inland convoying troop-carrying planes which in their turn . . ."

The voice petered out.

"It will begin again," said the deaf man hopefully. "I listened to the first part of it. It seems that they have brought a mixed force this time, with a lot of Japs amongst them. Their warships are shelling the city too; they got right up the coast under cover of night though nobody seems very clear as to where they came from."

"It all sounds dreadfully familiar," said Mr. Dale. "It's not only part of the tactics they used against Britain, but the phraseology is the same."

The little set came to life again with some hurried mutterings in Spanish. Then the announcer in English:

"We apologize for a technical hitch. I will repeat the last words. Convoying troop-carrying planes which in their turn appear to have made successful landings in the Californian desert, notably around Palm Springs where according to the latest reports the main engagement is taking place. As previously reported a number of Japanese troops is included, though it is impossible to state the proportion or even the total of the enemy force which has gained this footing, we hope only temporarily, on the territory of the United States. It must however be announced that hostile reinforcements are arriving hourly and that although equivalent reinforcements of American troops are likewise being rushed to the scene, a decision must not be expected with too great an impatience."

"That sounds bad," said Mr. Dale. "We shall next hear that American troops are withdrawing to more favourable positions. But why the devil do they want to go to Palm Springs? Is it a diversion? Are they intending to make a number of such diversions all over the States? After all, the American army can't be everywhere at once and it has got a large country to defend. The enemy has the advantage of surprise: he knows where he means to arrive next and we don't. It was inconvenient enough in our tiny Britain when they turned up in places where they were least expected. Well, it's no good wondering, but it sounds as though they meant business and I suppose we shall have to listen to the next bulletins."

§

The next bulletins were not re-assuring and it began to look as though Mr. Dale's conjecture might be right. The earlier landings had been on a much smaller scale, almost in the nature of reconnaissance, but it became increasingly evident that this attack was the real thing. Indifferent to their own losses, German and Japanese divisions descended from the skies in their thousands, and, since the whole of that vast land could not be covered everywhere by defensive units, it usually happened that they had ample time to assemble their tanks and set their artillery in position before the Americans could embarrass them with anything more than aircraft —and against that form of hindrance the enemy was naturally well protected. The enemy moreover appeared to be excellently informed as to the whereabouts of American troops and thus contrived to descend hundreds of miles away from the nearest concentration. It was even more bewildering than the sudden assault of the Japanese in December 1941, for it had come out of what seemed to be a peaceful sky.

Those who were dwelling at the bottom of the canyon listened dutifully to the reports coming through from Buenos Aires or any other station they could get, friendly or hostile. (The North American stations remained silent, and no official explanation was given, but it was hinted several times that they had all been put out of working order by traitorous activities.) They listened dutifully, but rather as though the whole thing were as unreal as a happening on another planet; rather as though they had brought the listening habit with them from another life. It was indeed curious to observe how some of these habits persisted, and also certain characteristics in each one, things which could not be dropped at once although they might be undergoing a noticeable modification day by day. Thus though Madame de Retz had become fully aware of the absurdity of her former profession and could even extract a lot of good fun from her surviving ledger, she still could never catch sight of Princess Irma without a sigh for the wasted possibilities of that perfect complexion. Mr. Dale said that at last he was beginning to believe in Purgatory, that reputedly transitional state. But the person whom Mrs. Temple noticed with the greatest interest was Loraine Driscoll. In the old days, which had ceased ten days ago, the girl's face had been her constant study, with the contrast between its remarkable smoothness of outline and the torment of anxiety in the eyes in repose. With such smoothness and youth a lovely serenity should have resulted; not gaiety, no, that face could never have been gay; but there should have been an untroubled emptiness, with no more mystery than the sweet mystery of innocence. Of late it had seemed to Mrs. Temple that the haunted look was fading, to be replaced by a look of liberation which in its turn brought, not the insipid loveliness of maidenhood, but the greater beauty of an experience suffered and vanquished.

It was natural that she should observe Loraine, since the task of telling the girl about her brother's death still lay before her. It would not be the first time she had broken such a piece of news but she was relieved when Loraine herself took the matter out of her hands.

"Mrs. Temple, do you remember once I came to your room at the hotel? I didn't know how I had the courage. I brought you some poinsettias, as a pretext for coming."

"I remember very well. I thought it was very kind of you."

"You thought more than that, I know you did. You saw that I wanted to stay in your room and talk to you. You were quite right. For some reason you wouldn't let me. Perhaps you had heard some of my friends teasing me and saying that I had a crush on you?"

Helen laughed. "I promise you, Loraine, such an idea never once entered my head. I probably thought you wanted to ask my advice about something and that it wasn't my business. What would your parents have said to a strange Englishwoman trying to influence their daughter?"

"You couldn't have influenced me, because no one, not even you, can undo what has been done. In any case I should probably have told you nothing. I just wanted to get away from the others and their chatter which I was finding unbearable. I hadn't even a bedroom to myself where I could be sure of being left alone. Besides, I found a peculiar comfort in your presence; I had only to look at you to feel that nothing mattered so much as I thought it did. You seemed to restore my sanity."

"I am very sorry," said Helen, "very sorry indeed." She was wondering more than ever how she could add her bad news to the burden which this child already carried.

"It doesn't matter now." Again that liberated look crossed her face. "Things have changed so much, and one's point of view. One exaggerated so ludicrously the things which had no importance at all. I used to get glimmerings of understanding this, even *then*, whenever I looked at you, Mrs. Temple, but of course the understanding comes more frequently now and before very long I think it will be permanent."

"Dear child, you are being rather cryptic. Don't think I want you to tell me anything you would rather not tell me. . . ."

"I am sure you don't; that would not be like you. And for your part, don't think either that I want to hold any secret against you. There is no secret of my life that I would not willingly tell you, but any confidence I could make would sound so small and crude in words now that the terror has gone. I suppose it is the terror one puts into things that gives them their significance; nothing exists, but thinking makes it so. I was miserable and frightened, but even through my wretchedness I used to sense a certain . . . splendour that made the horror almost beautiful. Oh, I don't know if you can understand what I mean. Reading Euripides used to give me the same sensation,—and it really was a sensation, rather than a thought,—like a shiver running over me, very transient,— and I always felt that if only I could seize it, hold it, look at it, I should learn and understand. Then to apply such . . . such intimations to myself was overwhelming; and I did so through no vainglory, believe me, but because that curious sensation caught me again and again in all its familiarity; I couldn't refuse to recognize it, but this time it was *me*, not Orestes, not Electra."

Mrs. Temple wondered slightly at the choice of characters. Brother and sister, she thought; brother and sister? . . .

"I might compare it," Loraine went on, "to someone

who wasn't thinking about ghosts, someone in broad
daylight, busy with quite ordinary things, who suddenly
looks up and sees the well-known figure standing there,
but only for a second; no sooner seen, than it is gone. The
only difference was that I saw nothing; I only felt."

"And you were quite unable to define this sensation
as you call it?"

"I often tried to. Then a queer thing happened. I
seemed to enter on to a third stage. It had begun with
Euripides and then it had transferred itself to myself, and
finally it seemed to comprise everyone in the whole
world. That was when I began to be afraid of losing my
sanity. I could understand being moved by the Greek
stories, I could even understand being . . . upset about
myself after . . . a certain thing which had happened to
me; but it scared me when I began to have the same
feeling, quite as definitely, on this gigantic scale. I haven't
much of a brain, Mrs. Temple, and it scared me to feel
that some appalling responsibility was being put upon me
and that I wasn't equipped to meet it."

"Responsibility?"

"I can only put it like this," said Loraine. "I felt that
some piece of knowledge was being dangled before me
and kept only just out of my reach. I felt that it was of
major importance that I should seize it and yet I couldn't;
my brain hadn't the swiftness or the strength. There were
other times when I thought it wasn't a question of brain
at all but of some other faculty, and I didn't seem to
possess that either."

"I think you are probably right there," said Mrs.
Temple, who had been following with great attention;
"it wasn't a question of brain."

"The nearest I ever got to a definition," said Loraine,
"was when I thought I must have an over developed
sense of jynx—oh, you look startled. Perhaps I shouldn't
have used that word. But really it was like that. You see,

I had had bad luck myself, and it seemed I had always known something bad was coming to me, and then when I began to feel the same way about all the millions on earth, well, I worried it round to the least alarming word I could find. You know how one does try to diminish anything one is frightened of."

"Tell me," said Mrs. Temple, "did you ever talk to anyone about things? To your brother, for instance?"

She had wanted to see the effect of this, and she saw it. Loraine could not turn pale since she was so pale by nature already, but she stood quite motionless and stared as though momentarily in the grip of her old experience. Her beauty was surprising, her pallor framed in the pale gold satin hair falling like a short wimple to her shoulders.

"To Robert?" she said. "Never. It is strange that you should ask, for I often wondered whether Robert was not made the same. You know what he was like. I suppose you all thought him the typical spoilt young American, too good-looking and too rich. So he was. And yet I wonder."

"Did you love your brother, Loraine?"

"Love him? I hated him as no one has ever been hated. It was a hatred that was very like love. Now I will tell you part of the truth, Mrs. Temple. Robert fascinated me as I fascinated him; we couldn't escape from one another; there was this dreadful, dreadful affinity which makes me believe that inside his damned spirit he was the same as I was. Curst. I sometimes thought we both were; and whenever I thought that, the same funny feeling overcame me; I told you I always recognized it when it came; there was no mistaking it. It came over me always when I thought of Robert in relation to myself."

"I don't quite understand," said Mrs. Temple, who was beginning to understand only too well.

"I don't understand either. I know only that it filled me with hatred and dread and poison. You see, it wasn't as though Robert had been the only loved pet at home always, or that our father and mother had spoilt him more than they spoilt me. They loved us both equally and they spoilt us both. They were rich, you see, and so they could afford to spoil us; there was no question of the boy getting the advantage over the girl in our family.— You've never met our parents, Mrs. Temple."

"No, but I have often thought about them. I have even made up stories about them in my mind, as I imagined them to be."

Loraine laughed. She had an attractive way of laughing; she threw her head back and the heavy gold hair fell back and the white throat came forward; but it was seldom that she had laughed at all.

"Oh, dear Mrs. Temple, I wonder what picture you have made about our parents in your mind? Some day you must tell me. But now, I am thinking only about Robert and me. He was my brother. It is the orthodox thing for a brother and sister to have a certain affection for one another, is it not? In spite of squabbles and nursery jealousies; when you are very young you throw toys at each other's heads and you compete for the place on your mother's lap; but between Robert and me it was never so simple. We never quarrelled in the nursery when we were small; we were as close and as loving as twins, although we weren't twins; it was only when we began to grow up that the tug began. Just now I said to you that I hated my brother. I used big words. I said hatred and dread and poison. All those words were true. It may seem odd to you to hear a girl using those words against a brother, when her relationship towards him ought to be a simple relationship, a natural relationship made up of the nursery and all the things they have in common, their home, their uncles and aunts, their cousins, their family jokes, the way the handle always comes off the tea-pot,—why, they ought to be able to

meet after a separation of twenty years and still join up
with such remembered links,—but instead of that, Mrs.
Temple, when I talk to you about my brother I use such
terrible words as hatred, dread, and poison, and I mean
them all as I speak them in their syllables one by one.
I hated my brother, I dreaded him and he poisoned me.
I hated him as I hope I shall never hate again; I loved
him as I hope I shall never love again.—I loved him, you
see, because I knew there was something fine in him
underneath the evil.—Oh yes, Mrs. Temple, don't wince
when I say evil. No one knows it better than I. There was
a streak of real evil in Robert, a streak of the real cruel
devil that hurts himself in order to hurt someone else; he
was a fallen angel. Poetic justice fulfilled its mission when
Robert like a falling angel got shot down from the sky."

With all her worldly wisdom Mrs. Temple found it
difficult to answer this tirade. So many things had been
packed into it, she would need some time to sort them
out. But the more immediate thing remained: Loraine
already knew that Robert was dead. It might be relatively
easy though distressing to tell a sister that her brother
had lost his life heroically in the defence of his country,
but with these extraordinary complications the task had
loomed more onerous even as it became more urgent.
Now Loraine had relieved her of it.

§

When Loraine had gone, Mrs. Temple sat thinking
over the curious story she had heard. It was not the kind
of story she usually welcomed, because it was the kind
of story that usually proceeded from self-conscious half-
informed people who wished to appear more interesting
than their fellows. She had heard many such, and experience had taught her to discount them. But Loraine was
different. Loraine was uninformed, she was puzzled, she

was artless; she had no idea of what she was really saying although she was groping all the time after the comprehension that eluded her; her very phraseology was touching in its mixture of polysyllables and colloquialisms. Jynx, she had said; and the little slang word coming instead of Destiny or Nemesis had been both convincing and pathetic. An over-developed sense of jynx. . . . It was not quite Cassandra's language perhaps ("Again upon me come the horrid pangs"), but the suffering seemed very much the same.

Mrs. Temple was perplexed. She was out of her depth. She wished that she might share the story and her perplexity with someone, for choice with Mr. Dale. She switched her thoughts away from Loraine to wonder why she should wish to share the story with anyone, and why in particular with that funny fat little man whom she had known for little more than a week. It was not her habit to want to share anything with anybody. She supposed it was because she could depend on him not to misunderstand anything she might say. She could in fact imagine exactly the conversation they would have and the remarks he would make. It startled her to discover how accurately she could estimate their conversation; it seemed that she already knew all his reactions instinctively. He would listen to her very gravely, without interrupting. Then a horrid suspicion would cross his mind, and he would say "You aren't going to tell me that you believe in reincarnation?" and she would remind him that at a very early stage of their acquaintance she had assured him that she believed neither in numerology, nor in the prophecy of the Pyramids. She had assured him definitely that she was not that sort of woman. Then he would look relieved and would say, "But . . . Electra and Orestes and all that? You aren't going to tell me next that Loraine and Robert Driscoll have murdered their mother? Dear me, I remember you drawing me an imaginary portrait of Mrs. Driscoll some days ago, and she didn't seem at all the sort of person to get herself murdered by her son and daughter. There was nothing of Clytemnestra about Mrs. Driscoll as you portrayed her."

She knew Mr. Dale well in this mood, but she knew also that a moment later he would be taking the thing seriously, with no jokes. "I see," he would say, rubbing his fingers over his chin in a familiar gesture as though to ascertain whether he had shaved properly that morning; "I see. You aren't trying to palm off any reincarnation stuff on me, but you are trying to suggest that mythology may repeat itself. You are telling me that Loraine and Robert were fated siblings, even as Electra and Orestes were fated. You are telling me that your pretty Loraine has had the curse of Cassandra put upon her, with this difference, that Cassandra prophesied and wasn't believed, but Loraine has all the intimations of prophecy and can't express it because she doesn't know clearly enough what she is intended to foresee. An uncomfortable position for a prophet.—Still, I see no inherent impossibility in your theory. I cannot see why an ancient legend should not repeat itself in these days. There is not much to be said for these days, perhaps, but at least we can say that they are on the heroic scale. We may not like the times we live in, but they do compare very favourably with that potty little affair they had at Troy. It is flattering to reflect that we are privileged to live in an age where everything is over life-size."

Then, Mrs. Temple thought, he would go in in his characteristic way to develop his argument. "You remember the legend," he would say, "the legend that a serpent wreathed itself round the body of Cassandra as she lay one night in the temple of Apollo, and by licking her ears gave her a knowledge of futurity. If I am not mistaken, her brother was involved in the same adventure. Brothers and sisters seem to have been particularly

favoured in classical times, so why not now? There may
indeed be something strange about this ordinary little
Driscoll pair. The only classical damnation they seem to
have escaped is incest . . ." and so he would ramble on,
and Mrs. Temple found herself sitting quite lost in her
imaginings about Mr. Dale. She could not see her own
face, but in fact she was wearing a smile of vague but
very real affection. It was odd, how fond she had become
of that fat little man. Odd, and rather touching. She had
gone through half a century of life without meeting
anybody whose mind pleased her own mind so closely.
It revived her belief in the potential happiness of life to
discover that after half a century of loneliness and of
human relationships going wrong, one could still unexpectedly find a person whose mental atmosphere exactly
matched one's own. That was a pleasant discovery to
make, so no wonder that Mrs. Temple sat with the
Colorado river rushing past her feet, smiling rather
sentimentally over the thought of Mr. Dale.

But suddenly another thought stung her, as though she
had been bitten by a rattlesnake. In the imagined conversation she had had with Mr. Dale, she had made him say,
"The only classical damnation they have escaped is
incest. . . ."

She was a morally brave and unconventional woman,
but that idea made her get up and walk quickly back
towards Phantom Ranch. "Oh Lord," she thought to
herself as she hurried towards the security of human
habitation, "Oh Lord, I do hope he is right. I wonder?
I wonder? Are there things in Loraine's life that she has
never told me about? Things that no girl would say?"

§

This was a suspicion too horrible to be shared even
with Mr. Dale, but she managed to thrust it out of her

mind, and to enjoy her friendship with him untroubled.
It sometimes seemed to her that it was becoming almost
as idyllic, though in a very different way, as the wandering
companionship between Louis and Jacqueline, for whenever she perceived him strolling towards her for the first
time in the morning her whole nature warmed to the
thought that she could now be with him again and that
the livelong day would be lit by the renewal of such
meetings. His company gave her a curious sense of
completion, and when he was not there she felt that
something was lacking, that something had gone cold
and grey and would return to life only when he reappeared. They did not always talk much. Their conversation came in bursts which might last for hours, since
there seemed to be so much they could talk about, and
so many by-ways of communication down which they
wanted to stray, so that their talk was always inconsistent,
rich and variegated, as though they never finished one
subject before they were darting off on another; but
equally they could sit silent for hours, or meander together
through the incredible kingdom they had been given to
explore, roving without fatigue or effort in a contentment
that neither of them had ever known. This exploration
of the canyon, at leisure, was a marvellous privilege to
have been given: it was *their* territory, *their* domain, in
its inexhaustible beauty and surprise. Loraine had said
that she used big words about her brother; but no words,
no superlatives were big enough to interpret the canyon
or to embrace its significance in a phrase. How little
those tourists could know, who descended the trail to
spend a few cheap hours at the bottom! It was necessary
to spend days, weeks, months, seasons, years, for its
magnitude and beauty fully to enlarge and enrich the
soul. This opportunity was theirs now, Helen's and Mr.
Dale's, with no pressure of life ahead of them, no rush,
no obligations, no term set to their long contemplation.

The luxury of eternal rest, eternal happiness, seemed to be offered to them as their portion.

He quoted a clerihew one day as they were sitting alone in a new place they had found, a ledge perched above the river. They had been sitting there in silence for a long time—but time did not count there, or then. "A lot of sense can be expressed in nonsense," he suddenly said, as though he had been following his own train of thought along its own rails without any regard for his companion or for what she herself might be thinking of. She liked him the better for this occasional indifference when he took no notice of her or of what she might be thinking. It meant that he was not subservient to her in any way and preserved his independence of thought and being. That was how she liked people to be, being made in the same mould herself. "A lot of sense expressed in terms of nonsense," he said. "Cammaerts once remarked that the English had a peculiarly well-developed talent for nonsense. He instanced Lewis Carroll and Lear as the supreme masters in this field. He might well have quoted Bentley as a successor to Lear and Lewis Carroll:

"What I like about Lord Clive
Is that he's no longer alive.
There's a lot to be said
For being dead."

It was the first time that either of them had alluded to the fact of their both being dead. They both felt so remarkably alive, more alive than they had ever felt in their ordinary lives before, that it was difficult to realize that they both had been killed by blast some ten days ago.

There was indeed a great deal to be said for being dead. It was much more pleasant to be dead than alive, if being dead meant that one gained this new angle of proportion on life. Any reasonable person would prefer to be dead than alive. So, Mrs. Temple and Mr. Dale wandered

among the immensities of the canyon with the peace and
certainty of being dead in their bodies. Their souls were
not dead; no soul could die. No soul could be killed. So,
it was their souls that met, not their bodies; it was their
spirit that met in the unfolding of such gradual beauty
as they shared together, but from time to time their eyes
met in a long look, a long silent gaze of understanding,
which in the course of time they came to recognize as a
union between them and called it their drollery.

It was Helen who invented this phrase. The first two
or three times this odd phenomenon happened between
them, she said nothing; he said nothing either; but the
fourth time it occurred, after they had gazed at one
another in silence and had felt a current running between
them, she said "Look here, this is very odd. It is a very
definite thing, so definite that we must have a word for
it. Let us call it our drollery, for it really is so very droll
that such a thing should come to such staid people as
you and me."

They did so call it, henceforward, as a joke, whenever
it occurred between them. They said nothing, they
needed not to say anything, but needed only to smile in
an understanding way. A glance was enough. They both
knew what had taken place.

It was not easily definable, and although it seemed
comparable to certain other states of human experience
Helen hesitated to draw the comparison, even to herself,
such was her dread of anything approaching the high-
falutin. Yet she was tempted to believe that a similar
almost trance-like mood possessed the artist in moments
of creative inspiration, the visionary on the brink of
revelation, the mystic in the hour of Union, with this
difference, that those experiences were passionately
lonely, whereas hers was shared. It was like a very prolonged, very quiet orgasm of the understanding instead
of the quick and quickly-forgotten orgasm of the senses;

N

and it was an understanding which comprised not only
their two selves, but every mystery latent in the invisible
universe.

She thought also that it came to them as definitely and
as regularly as Loraine's sense of futurity had come to
her. But, as she had still said nothing of this to Mr. Dale,
it being too private a thing, she said nothing of it now.
She was content to keep it to herself as a sort of double
secret which she might share with him did she choose to
do so. She would save that up for a later day. It made
love richer to have something saved up for a later day.
One did not give everything out at once. An essential of
love was to keep something in reserve always.

Love, she thought, as the word crawled for the first time
into her mind? Love? Oh no, not love for me, something
far older, far more veiled in the twilight than that; not
love, not that rash reckless thing, not that young thing,
not that thing enjoyed by Louis and Jacqueline, not that
ecstasy, that dashing of young body against young body,
not that, not that for me. For me, only the quiet thing;
only friendship, companionship; and God knows that is
all one can reasonably expect from life at our age and
after all the things we have both gone through. It might
be an unusual form of love, if love it could be called at
all, but why should love be so stereotyped, so orthodox
always? Why not have some diversion, some fugue on
the perpetual theme?

There was no sentimentality between them. They were
even rude to one another sometimes, and told one
another their faults bluntly. "You are a bore sometimes,
you know," said Mrs. Temple; "you think you know
about life, when you really don't know the A B C of it."
"And you," he would retort, "you set yourself up as the
wise woman when you don't know the A B C either."
Then they would both laugh and would both agree that
the other was right. It did not seem to matter whether

they understood the alphabet of life or not; what mattered
was that they understood each other and could share the
life-after-death as they were sharing it now.

§

Meanwhile, external life was tearing itself to pieces
round them and reached them by the unreal sort of
communication conveyed by the radio. There was a great
contrast between the private life of beauty they were
leading and the public hideous life that was going on
outside. Men were fighting and murdering each other
again as they had fought and murdered in the first
World War. Neither Mr. Dale nor Mrs. Temple could
see why. It seemed inexplicable to them why millions of
men should wish to fight other millions of men when the
obvious solution for all those millions of men sharing the
same planet lay in co-operation, both economic and
geographical. A fair distribution would give room to
everybody. The planet wasn't so overcrowded surely?
In certain areas there might be too many human beings
crushed into the square mile; there might be crops wasted
in one country while another country went short; but
surely both those problems might be adjusted by a little
intelligent agreement? Men couldn't be so foolish as to
fail over so simple, so elementary a thing, after all the
centuries they had been granted for development since
they first crept out from the mouth of their cave. Yet it
did seem that men so failed.

Man had shown himself ingenious in his inventions. He
had discovered that the earth went round the sun, not
the sun round the earth. By a series of complicated
mathematical calculations he had discovered the planet
Neptune and had also enabled himself to predict the
precise moment in which the sun or the moon would
enter into an eclipse. He had discovered more things than

these. He had found out the composition of the atom and had formulated certain theories about thermo-dynamics. He had made up an idea about the distribution of the known universe. All those were very difficult things to find out. The one thing he had never found out was how to deal with himself or with others of his kind.

He had invented a thing called "his enemies," and many means of destroying them. His enemies on their part had invented an equal number of means for destroying him. Planes and bombs grew swifter and more enormous; and every new invention was quickly capped by a newer invention which went one better. Yet, in spite of all this, man that clever creature, cleverer far cleverer than the ape, failed entirely over the one faculty that mattered, the faculty of being able to arrange his life in accordance with his fellows.

Could the world never be at peace? It seemed not.

It was not easy to grasp exactly what was going on in the world. The Buenos Aires wireless news seemed to be fairly reliable, but it had always to be checked by the broadcasts from the Axis powers. Berlin and Tokio were jubilant, and Rome of course followed their lead meekly. (It was more evident than ever that Italy had shrunk to a mere province of Germany.) The three stations talked freely about the anticipated end of the war, and boasted that owing to the complete surprise they had been able to spring on her, America would very soon be in a position where nothing would remain for her but to plead for peace. There were no exhortations this time to the people to keep up their courage and determination in spite of temporary reverses: no reverses were admitted, and indeed it appeared that none had been suffered. The Axis had simply swept down on the United States and had done precisely as they chose there. There was retaliation, of course. The American air-arm claimed tremendous damage on Tokio and Yokohama, which were more

vulnerable to high explosive and incendiary bombs than
the steel-and-concrete of American cities. But these were
minor successes. The fact remained that many thousands
of square miles of American territory were in the occupation of the enemy and that there seemed no possibility
of arresting the flood of reinforcements which came
pouring down from the sky.

Meanwhile what was happening in New York? They
had known for some days that a tremendous air and sea
battle was taking place, evidently as a development of the
naval action which had been previously reported off the
coast of Maine, in which, it may be remembered, two
American destroyers and two cruisers had been lost and
an equal number had been claimed against the enemy.
This, it now became apparent, had been nothing more
than a preliminary skirmish. The few German ships
engaged had been but the reconnoitering vanguard of
their entire Atlantic fleet, which, "on manœuvres" in
mid-ocean when war broke out, had now appeared in full
force off Manhattan. (How they had got safely through
the hastily sown mine-field nobody knew, nobody
stopped to enquire, but it was pretty obvious that they
had their informers ready on the spot.) The population
was appalled, those who were left and who could not start
trekking along the roads towards the relative safety of the
Alleghanies or the Berkshire hills. They were appalled
when the great shells from the naval guns came sailing
over in a trajectory which cleared the roofs of the highest
sky-scraper and fell to their explosion in the fissure of the
streets, naval guns whose reputation had preceded them
but whose existence had never quite been believed in,
even by the American Navy Department. The reverber-
ations of the shells produced more effect than the actual
damage they caused. The noise was almost more than
human nerves or ear-drums could endure, and made the
population feel as though the whole of their city was

going up, to descend after a slow-motion mid-air turn-over of masonry immediately again upon their heads. They took it, even as other cities had taken it; but it was a particularly high trial.

This was bad enough, when you added in the heavy air-bombing going on continuously all day and all night, on a scale that had never been known before, not even in the blitzes on the European cities. This war made the other war look like little boys playing at soldiers, as Mr. Dale had foreseen some days ago. The horrible strides in all mechanized objects had not altered, but only accelerated and intensified the character of everything all round. Machines went faster; explosions fell heavier; noise grew louder; bigger and better had been the slogan of man-kind, and now mankind was cashing the dividends of the investment it had made. Bigger, yes, but better? The citizens of proud New York doubted it as they covered their ears with their hands to shut out the din; and sat wondering whether it was preferable to be on the ground-floor or on the fifty-second.

§

This was battle indeed, in the modern sense of the term: a mixture of madness and organization. It seemed that the combat of civilization could go no further, could reach no higher peak of dread than in this whirling screaming vortex of warplanes over and between the skyscrapers of the towering city, where the defenders dashed among the attackers and both fell hurtling after the incessant bombs, and the bombers in the stratosphere rained explosives down too, regardless of what plane they might chance to hit below, and the guns of the two fleets and the shore-batteries crashed salvo after salvo in one undistinguishable roar, until there was no sanity left in the din and the speed and the destruction.

It was no longer possible even for the commanders to keep track of the casualties among their units. Nothing was a unit any more, but just one element in the vast confusion. Machines could no longer be estimated in squadrons; it was impossible to collate information; had a hundred planes been lost, or two hundred, or five? Had another battle-cruiser been sunk? The *Nuremberg*? The *Wisconsin*? The *Lohengrin*? The *Lincoln*? The *Nippon-maru*? The *Vittorio Emanuele*? No one had time to know. The curious fact, in all this murderous chaos, was the comparatively small loss of life. Airmen perished, and a number of sailors, but owing to the peculiar construction of buildings (which seemed now as though they had been designed expressly to resist such an attack) the civil population scarcely took harm. They speedily realized that no bomb ever made would go through more than thirty storeys, so, New York being what it was, the cowering civilians could keep their limbs though they might lose their reason.

The city presented a strange sight after the first day of battle. Fires had broken out on the top reaches, and Rockfeller Centre especially was a tiara of pointed flame, though the Empire State Building remained tall, black, and entire. London had burnt, but poor ancient London had been more inflammable than New York, and there had been nothing in London to give that diabolical effect of ringing flames so high up in the air.

Something of all this came through on the radio, though the accounts reflected something of the confusion also. But it was not until the battle had been going on for twenty-four hours that the first indication came of something even more seriously wrong. It seemed unbelievable that an even higher peak of terror could be reached but in spite of a caution of censorship imposed abruptly upon the radio the listeners at the bottom of the canyon realized that rumours improbable and wild beyond the nature of Rumour were flying as swiftly as the killer-planes. Buenos Aires gave out a hint; and, oddly enough, Berlin, Tokio and Rome also gave out hints within the hour: it was the first time that all these stations had ever struck the same note, as though something stronger than their own warring interests had taken charge and was forcing them into collaboration. "Something very odd indeed has happened or is happening," said Mr. Dale, who had been listening to the broadcast with more interest than he usually displayed. "Come along, Helen, let us go for a walk. We can either think about it or else dismiss it from our minds. The deaf man isn't here, he has gone to look for squirrels, so I shall put his neat little set into my pocket. Come along."

§

It was thus that they heard the first full account of the most extraordinary battle so far recorded in terrestrial history. It was as though the radio stations had independently decided to save it up until a full account could be given; as though they had all shrunk from imposing anything so awesome upon humanity before complete confirmation had been received. Even then the announcement began cautiously, the announcement coming with the voice of the still sober world beyond the mad focus of New York.

"For some days now," the voice began, "any communication with New York has been hard to establish, and only the daring of a few war-correspondents who ventured in chartered planes to dash round that inferno has provided us with any news that we could regard as reliable. Now, however, survivors of the incredible catastrophe have begun to arrive at various points of refuge, and it is from their verbal accounts that we are at last able to construct some kind of picture. It has been our policy to refuse credence to the rumours which had begun to filter through, but it is now no longer possible to preserve our reticence in view of the evidence which is now overwhelming and agrees in a remarkable degree with such details as had been hitherto available. This agreement is all the more impressive considering the mental distress from which the witnesses are naturally suffering.—One moment, please. Stand by."

"I wish he would come to the point," said Mr. Dale. "I do not believe it was in the least necessary to ask us to stand by just then. He does it partly to annoy and partly because he is enjoying himself thoroughly, licking his chops somewhere in the safety of the Argentine. He realizes that this is one of the high-light moments of his little second-hand form of life and he has every intention of making it go as far as he can."

"Oh, *do* be quiet," said Mrs. Temple.

"Like all women," said Mr. Dale, "you have no sense of occasion. You evidently have no artistry in your soul. You do not appreciate the value of suspense. That announcer in Buenos Aires does. He is an artist in his peddling way even as Royer was an artist in his. I respect that unknown man for making us wait. I marvel only that he doesn't fill up the interval with a gramophone record, Adelina Patti singing "Home, Sweet Home" for instance. Homes are so sweet these days, aren't they, so secure, so invulnerable from outside attack, that our announcer should surely celebrate them by that little ditty. All the same, I confess to some curiosity concerning what he is going to say when he is so obliging as to begin speaking again. I dislike his style in his use of the English language, but that no doubt is to be blamed on someone else, not on him. Never mind about that. I daresay that my criticism is irrelevant and that such niceties should be shelved to await a more propitious time. It is relevant, however, to remind you during this pause to which we are both listening, if one may properly be said to be listening to a pause, that during the last war some philosophically minded wits suggested that nothing but the approach of a disorderly star involving the total destruction of this planet or, failing that, a terrestrial invasion by the inhabitants of some other planet revolving within our own small solar system, would bring the warring inhabitants of earth to their senses. Both those solutions were suggested, so, as I remarked just now, it may not be irrelevant to remind you of them when something of the sort may be occurring. . . ."

"Mr. Dale, once already I have asked you to keep quiet. There are moments when I find you intolerable, and this is one of them. So will you please stop playing games with your imagination and your irony? That tiny invention which is lying on the rock between us is about to start talking again. The buzz is coming through and I want to listen if you will kindly allow me to do so."

> "We apologize for the delay. We were saying when transmission was temporarily interrupted that the agreement between witnesses was most impressive. We can no longer refuse the facts.
>
> "Here they are.
>
> "New York City as listeners already know was heavily attacked by hostile air-fleets three days ago, a naval battle raging in conjunction. We will not repeat the description of either of those battles. We have an even more serious eventuality to report. It has long been known to geologists that New York City and indeed the whole strip of the eastern sea-board stood upon a seismic zone; in plain English, an earthquake zone, a geological fault. The rocks upon which New York was constructed were known to be shallow, but no recorded earth-tremor of any importance had occurred since the New England earthquake of 1874. It has occurred now. In the midst of the man-made battle raging overhead, Nature as though outraged has bestirred herself to take her part.

An earthquake of unparalleled violence has shaken the eastern coasts of the United States from New Haven to Cape May, and its centre of disturbance was located under the heart of New York City itself.

"The consequences have yet to be fully estimated. It is already known however that owing to the subsidence of the rocky strata, the tall buildings have toppled sideways and are now leaning against one another at varying angles. It is said for example that the Chrysler Building is propping itself against the opposite side of the street.

"It is of course due to the method of construction of the tall buildings that they have not entirely collapsed but have merely swayed and finally come to rest against one another. Steel and concrete have a certain elasticity. The effect as described by one observer from the air must be grotesque in the extreme.

"It is reported also that a rift has appeared in the earth running the whole length of what was once Fifth Avenue. The observer who reported this fact (which we accept with reservation) commented that the gash thus created reminded him of a section of the Grand Canyon of the Colorado. He said that he seemed to look as deep into the earth, and that the tumbled masonry of the buildings suggested the natural rock formation of that region.

"It seems certain that a tidal wave of unprecedented dimensions followed upon the catastrophe, and that a number of the warships which were engaged in combat off the coast were lifted by the wall of water and dashed upon the shore, irrespective of their nationality.

"It is not known for certain what has happened to the legions of air-craft which at the moment when the catastrophe occurred were engaged in combat over the city. We are unable to state whether they have landed in order to take part in rescue-work or whether they are pursuing their task of destroying one another.

"That is the end of the present bulletin."

§

When the voice had ceased, and the deafening chords had died away, Helen and Mr. Dale looked at each other in silence. They could not immediately take in the thing they had heard; it lay too far outside experience, and they both knew well that the human heart could accept manifold suffering only in the measure of its own unit. Physical events, however terrible, however multiple, were neither larger nor smaller than the capacity of the heart to interpret them. That was what dwarfed the physical event and made it meaningless. It had, in itself, no significance; the significance lay only in what it symbolized.

As though they recognized their incapacity, they made no attempt to encircle the facts as facts. They had heard with their ears, and now they were looking at each other with their eyes, but neither their senses nor their intelligence seemed to have any connexion with what was going on in a more important region of their inner selves. They stared themselves into a daze, so that they became as people mesmerized, yet at the same time an awareness came to them, as valid and unequivocal as a great spiritual experience. They felt, they saw, and they understood. Very gradually the thing they called their drollery came to them. It came stealing over them like a thing arriving in slow motion. It came like a stillness creeping across the clangour of the outside world, a stillness which yet contained some quality of music. They said nothing, but held each other's souls in that long deep look which had nothing to do with ordinary love, though love was included in it as indeed all things were included.

When they did begin to return to consciousness, when their drollery slowly receded, as it always did after the few intense seconds of its domination, they began to speak again in lowered voices. The lowering had nothing to do with the occurrence of their curious communion. They did not even refer to any personal event between them. Their few remarks were not concerned with personal matters, but were cast more in the soft chords of a final requiem. Mr. Dale had quite abandoned his bantering tone; he spoke with extreme gentleness and gravity.

"How beautiful the cliffs are in this evening light," he said; "how beautiful, and how different from the broken tops of those shattered cities.—So Nature has taken a hand at last, to help on the destruction imagined by man to wreak on his brothers. It will be called the intervention of Providence, but even the Churches will be hard put to it to say on whose behalf Providence intended to intervene, since those ships were flung indiscriminately ashore and along the beaches lie the drowned seamen of many nations. Providence has given only a further proof of her grand impartiality. She might as easily have submerged the entire Japanese archipelago. And what will be the effect on the mind of man? My friend, it will take more than a mere earthquake to bring about a change of heart. The battle is not yet over, for the battle rages between darker forces than the warplane and the gun. Terrible in their execution, they are no more than the machine obedient to the far more terrible dementia of their masters. Earth will have shaken her locks in vain, and not until she has shaken this whole race off into the void will peace return. Or do I mistrust too much? Just now I saw so clearly. Is it after all possible that some vision of sanity may come through the clouds, not in a miraculous blinding, but in a pervasive dawning that will bring understanding between soul and soul and peace between nation and nation? Helen, you and I, since we have passed the frontier of death and are now immortal, will see that day. It is for those who will not see it that I sorrow; those who will continue to live in the conviction that their present folly is permanent and irremediable."

"Do not forget," she said, "that to them also an hour will come when they have to cross the frontier of death, and that then, like us, they may live on to see that other day."

"Meanwhile," he said, "let us go, Helen; let us walk in this place where there is no misunderstanding. Where there is nothing but beauty and comprehension, those two smothered elements which hide in all souls and are so seldom allowed to find their way to the surface. Here we are purified. Is it indeed necessary that man should die, in order to uncover the meaning of life? It seems so.— Let us go, Helen. Shall we stroll up the river towards its source, or down the river towards the sea? Whichever direction we choose, we shall not get very far, for the source is many hundreds of miles away and so is the sea, and in either direction the route is stopped by rocks and rapids. We shall not get very far. We know that other mountains and other hills shall in time be washed into the sea, and coral reefs and shales and bones and disintegrated mountains shall be made into beds of rock, for a new land where new rivers shall flow. But in the meantime let us enjoy the strip of beauty that has been granted to us."

They trusted one another, and in serenity and confidence they went.